CHRISTMAS DAYS

Christmas Days

BY JOSEPH C. LINCOLN

ILLUSTRATED BY HAROLD BRETT

New York

COWARD-McCANN, INC., 1938

Typography by Robert Josephy

CONTENTS

PART ONE

The Fifties

PART ONE

THE FIFTIES

I

THE BOYS were in the woods back of Sandy
Pond hunting for evergreen and hog cranberry. The evergreen—it had other names,
but no one on the Cape ever called it anything but
evergreen—grew in the open spaces between the
pitch pine and scrub oaks. It twined and twisted in

and out under and amid the pine needles and dead leaves, and you pulled it out in long streamers. Its foliage looked like that of the arbor vitæ trees on Grandfather's lot in the cemetery and had the same spicy odor. The hog cranberry—why "hog" nobody seems to know—was almost like the real cranberry, except that the berries were not as pretty and were unfit to eat. It, too, grew close to the ground, and there were places where it covered the grass and moss for yards and yards like a thick green mat. Almost everyone gathered evergreen and hog cranberry at Christmas time. They made wreaths of the former and long festoons of the latter to hang in the front parlor and sitting-room and dining-room, especially if "company" was expected.

Thanksgiving had always been the festival season in Puritan New England, and it was yet to the majority of Bayporters; but to the Days—even Grandfather Captain Elijah Day and Grandmother Olivia —to them, and to their children and grandchildren, Christmas was the season of family reunion. Even before Grandfather retired from the sea, when, after his third lucky voyage in command of a whaler, he spent the larger portion of his profits in building the white-clapboarded, brick-ended, green-blinded house on the main road in Bayport—1832 that was—even then he said to Grandmother: "Well, there she is,

'Livia. And there I hope she'll be for a good long spell—home, by the everlasting! Home for you and me and the young-ones and their young-ones after 'em. I tell you, my girl, there's nothing like a stretch of three-year voyages up North, three years at a time of wet and ice and grease and smells and salt-horse and hardtack, to make a fellow appreciate what home means. Maybe our boys won't have that kind of training, but you and I must do our best to pump the home feeling into 'em and see that it sticks there."

Grandmother Olivia sighed. To her mind there was little doubt as to the kind of training in store for her sons. Isaac, the elder, was already at sea, mate of a Hong Kong-bound bark; and Edgar, the younger, was fretting because he must spend another year in school before embarking on his first voyage under a Bayport captain. Olivia would not have wished it otherwise, of course. Her boys were, as they should be, ambitious and eager to get on in the world, and, for a Cape Cod boy of that period, the broad ocean was the highway to success.

But that was early in the thirties. Now, twenty years later, the children in the woods in search of evergreen and hog cranberry were Elijah and Olivia's grandchildren. They were Edgar's sons. Isaac had been dead for fifteen years, washed overboard in a typhoon in the Java Sea, and Edgar and his wife—

Martha Snow was her maiden name—were somewhere between Liverpool and Boston, bound for the latter port. Edgar was captain of the ship *White Foam* and Martha was with him. The two sons, Rogers, the elder, and David, two years younger, had remained ashore with their grandparents and were attending school in the village.

Rogers, tall for his age, broad-shouldered, a Day every inch of him, pulled a long streamer of evergreen from beneath the pine needles and tossed it into the clothesbasket they had brought with them.

"That's enough," he declared. "All we can lug, anyhow. If Grandma and 'Relia want more let 'em send somebody else for it. Come on, Dave, catch hold of the other handle."

David rose from the hog cranberry patch where he had been grubbing, picked up the heap of glossy, green-leaved vines he had accumulated and added it to the contents of the brimming basket. He was not as tall as his brother, nor as stockily built. Rogers' hair was black, and his was a light brown. Rogers' eyes were brown and David's a blue-gray. Dave took after his mother's people, the Snows—everybody said so.

Carrying the clothesbasket between them, they walked through the woods, over the knoll and down across the field to the road where Major, the white horse, stood dozing between the shafts of the blue-painted "truck wagon." Grandfather Day owned two horses, but Major was the older and "safer." He would "stand without hitching," welcomed the chance to stand anywhere and for any length of time, which was why the boys were permitted to drive him. They—Rogers particularly—resented the discrimination. "Nick," the other horse, was young, liked to trot, and picked up his feet prettily when he stepped. Nick had some style to him, whereas Rogers' name for Major was "the old cow."

The clothesbasket was lifted in over the tailboard of the truck wagon, the blanket was removed from the horse's back and folded lengthwise on the seat to serve as a cushion, the boys climbed aboard, Rogers picked up the reins, and, after the customary amount of persuasion, Major consented to move forward at a dignified walk.

The road, two parallel foot-deep furrows in the yellow sand with strips of briars, dead grass and low bushes and a "horsepath" in the middle, wound around the edge of the pond and up the hill beyond. Sandy Pond—there were pickerel and yellow and white perch in it—looked steely-gray and forbidding in the December afternoon light. The fields were bare, the trees—except the pines, of course—were leaf-less, the sky was a slaty gray, the wind, as they came to the top of the little hill, was raw and damp and chill. Rogers pulled his cap down over his ears and tightened the woolen tippet about his neck.

"Feels like snow," he declared. "Thoph said 'twould snow before morning. Shouldn't wonder if he was right."

Dave slapped his mittened hands across his chest to warm them.

"Snow on Christmas would be fun," he announced, with enthusiasm.

Rogers sniffed. "Why?" he asked. "Like shoveling out, do you? Maybe Grandpa'll give you a snow shovel for Christmas, if you asked him. If he gives me one you can have it and welcome."

Dave grinned rather sheepishly. He was accustomed to being snubbed by his big brother. It was something to be noticed by him; there were fellows in school who would give a good deal for even that much attention from Rog Day.

"Oh, I don't know," he said. "Shoveling isn't so bad, if there isn't too much of it. You used to like it, anyhow you said you did."

"Maybe. I used to like scratching for hog cranberry and evergreen vines, but I'm getting sick of that, too. It's kid's stuff, and I'm no kid nowadays. I'm sick of home, far's that goes."

"Sick of home!" Dave was horrified. "What's the

matter with home? There aren't many fellows with a better home than we've got. No, nor better folks than Grandma and Grandpa—yes, and Ma and Pa, too, when they're home. Gee, I wish they'd get home for Christmas! Maybe they will. I heard Grandpa say he hadn't given up hope of it. Don't you wish they would, Rog?"

"Course I do. But I'd rather be where they are now than home, Christmas or any other time. That's where I want to be. Yes, and I'm going to be before very long. Look at it!"

They had reached the top of the hill, and on the other side and below was Bayport, with its clusters of houses, its spreading leafless elms and silver-leaf poplars and, beyond it, stretching to the horizon, the sea. It was at the sea Rogers was pointing.

"That's where I belong," he said. "I'm sick of studying and all that young-one stuff. I want to get aboard a vessel and learn navigating and things. I'm going to cap'n a ship of my own by the time I'm twenty-one. Pa did, and so did Grandpa. There hasn't been a Day forever and ever that didn't go to sea, I bet. . . . Well, why don't you say something? You're a Day, same as I am. Don't you mean to go to sea yourself some day?"

Dave drew a long breath. "Course I do," he replied solemnly. "Rather do it than anything in the world. Only—"

"Only what?"

"Only what's the use of talking about it now? We can't go yet awhile; they won't let us."

Rogers laughed. "Won't, eh?" he said. "No, they won't let you, that's right enough. But I shouldn't wonder if they let me. Ye-es"—with a nod that signified much—"I shouldn't wonder at all."

Dave turned on the seat. He regarded his brother earnestly. "What do you mean, Rog?" he asked.

"Mean what I say. I've heard 'em talking—Grandpa and Grandma—when they thought I wasn't around. Cousin Fred's coming down for Christmas. You knew that, though; course you did."

"Um-hm. He and Emmie are coming. So's Cousin Bailey and Cousin Sarah and Jeddie and Aunt Desire Snow. They'll all be here for dinner Christmas Day. What of it?"

"Nothing of it, so far as Cousin Bailey and his tribe go. They don't amount to anything, nor Aunt Desire neither. But Cousin Fred's different; he amounts to a whole lot. He's a big shipping merchant, Cousin Fred is. One of the big ones up in Boston. He and his partner own ships, clippers, some of 'em. Why, McKay"—he spoke the famous shipbuilder's name with reverence—"built the *Spread Wing* purpose for Cousin Fred's firm. And you know what a record *she's* made."

"Course, everybody that knows anything about ships knows that. Fastest passage between California and Boston. Carried away her fore-topmast in a gale off Cape Horn, too, and in spite of that she made the trip and beat 'em all. Cap'n John Marvin commanded her that voyage. Godfreys! I'd like to have been aboard!"

His eyes were shining. Rogers was evidently surprised at his enthusiasm.

"Huh!" he grunted. "Do know something about it, after all, don't you? Didn't suppose you cared for vessels and such the way I do. You never talk about 'em much. But then"—loftily—"you wouldn't, I suppose. Maybe I didn't when I was your age."

There was a scant two years' difference between their birthdays, but two years at that period of life are long indeed. Dave was quite aware of the fact.

"What about Cousin Fred and you?" he asked.

"Considerable, boy, and don't you forget it. I've been teasing Grandpa to let me go to sea, been keeping at him every chance I've got, but he wouldn't pay attention; talked about my finishing my schooling and all that rot. Schooling!" he said contemptuously. "How much schooling did he have? Went cabin boy on the old *High Flyer*, with Cap'n Ezra Baker, when he was only eleven. Eleven, mind you! Anyhow, when I went up to Boston last September with Grandpa we were in Cousin Fred's office a lot of times, and I asked Grandpa about my going to sea right in front of Cousin Fred. They laughed, but I bet you they talked about it afterwards. Fact is, I know they did."

"How do you know?"

"Because the other night I heard Grandpa and Grandma talking together in the sitting-room after they thought I'd gone to bed. Grandpa said something about Fred's folks—the firm, I mean—fitting out a vessel for a voyage to Leghorn. That's in—in—"

"It's in Italy. Pa went there four years ago; don't you remember? He brought home that big jar of tamarind preserve from there. And he brought Ma—"

"Yes, yes. I know all that. Well, I heard Grandpa say that Cap'n Seabury, from right here in West Bayport, was to have that ship when she sailed, and he was looking for a likely cabin boy. Then Grandma said: ''Lijah, you're not thinking of letting him have our Rogers, are you? I know he's crazy to get on salt water, but—oh, dear me, he's so young!' Grandpa said: 'He isn't as young as I was—no, nor his father was—when we broke in. Of course, I shouldn't do it without Edgar and Martha's consent, but if they *should* get here pretty soon, why, we might talk it over with 'em, mightn't we? Dave Seabury is an able shipmaster and he'd treat a boy right.' That's what he said, I heard him. . . . Gosh!"

He paused. Dave said "Gee!" Both boys were silent for a moment, their thoughts far away from Bayport and Christmas and evergreens, all that was prosaically associated with dry land and familiar sights and happenings. Then Rogers remembered.

"Say," he ordered sharply, "don't you tell anybody what I just told you. If you do—"

"Course I won't. Grandpa wouldn't like it if he knew you listened."

"Didn't listen. I just heard."

"Well, I won't tell, anyhow."

Another interval of silence, unbroken save by the "plop, plop" of old Major's feet on the frozen ground. They had left the rutted lane now and were on the main road. This time David spoke first.

"Cousin Fred's bringing Emmie with him," he said. "That's kind of too bad. Now there's got to be a girl hanging round, spoiling everything."

Rogers laughed. "Doesn't sound too bad to me," he observed. "You haven't seen Emmie lately, have you? Well, I have. She's—she's—well, wait till you do see her, that's all. Emmie's grown up."

"Grown up! What do you mean? She isn't any

older than I am. Just the same age, we are. Heard Grandma say so the other day."

The statement was indisputably true, and for the moment it served to take the older brother rather aback.

"Why—well, yes, I suppose maybe she is," he admitted reluctantly. "Yes, guess that's so, when you come to think of it. But—well, anyhow, she seems older, almost as old as I am. She and I saw a good deal of each other when I was up to Boston. Grandpa and I stayed two days and nights at Cousin Fred's, you know. Gosh, what a house that is! Pictures—and—and everything."

"We've got pictures here in our house."

"Not that kind of pictures, we haven't. Hand-painted ones. 'Bay of Naples' and 'Rock of Gibraltar' and Emily's mother before she was married—oh, every kind. You ought to see 'em, boy."

David devoutly wished he might. He had made but two trips to Boston in his life, one when he was four and the other three years later. Rogers had made the trip to the big city five times, his latest visit this very year. Big brothers were lucky. The younger ones had to take what was left. He changed the subject.

"Don't see what difference Emmie's being as old as I am makes," he said. "She's a girl, just the same."

The contempt in the statement was not quite sincere. David was beginning to notice girls, just a little. He was a shy boy, but a real boy nevertheless. Girl ways and girl plays had never appealed to him, but during the past two years he had changed slightly. Of course, being a boy, and particularly a country boy, he had heard all sorts of things about the feminine sex, and his grandmother would have been shocked and surprised at the extent of his knowledge. It was only recently, however, that he had begun to realize how much nicer some girls were to look at than others and how some of them—one or two of the Bayport girls in particular—had a way that—that kind of made a fellow like to be with them.

He wouldn't have mentioned this to a soul, least of all to his brother, who would have made fun of him. Rogers was quite a chap for the girls nowadays. Went to parties—late parties, eleven o'clock before he got home sometimes—and on hay-rides, saw girls home from prayer-meetings and from singing school —was a squire of dames, in fact, or hoped he was. And the girls liked him, too. David was inclined to be diffident and sensitive, blushed when there was nothing to blush for, and was decidedly not the life of the few parties he had attended. Nevertheless, although the girls did not notice him particularly, he was beginning to notice them. And, to cover up this budding notice, he pretended to be scornfully contemptuous of the sex.

Rogers, however, was not aware of the pretense. His brother was a kid, that's all, and spoke and thought like one.

"You bet Emmie's a girl," he said, with a significant nod. "And there's no girl in this town that's in the same class with her. You just wait."

"Is she prettier than Susie Taylor?" naming Bayport's leading example of juvenile feminine beauty.

"Prettier? Ha! You wait till you see. And she's different, too."

"How different?"

"Oh, I don't know. Can't tell you how, but she is. She and I are mighty good friends," he said complacently. "Yes, and we're going to be better. Someday, if I have luck— Oh, well, you may not be glad she's coming here for Christmas, but *I* am."

He began to whistle. Major jogged along the main road, past the old First Meeting House and the town hall and the Come-Outer chapel, and halted before the entrance to the Day driveway. Dave climbed from the seat to unhook the chain between the granite posts of the drive. Even there in the yard there was an aroma of spice and molasses and hot stove in the air. Grandma and Aurelia, the hired girl, were in the kitchen making Christmas cookies.

2

THOPH TIDDITT—he was christened Theophilus, but he had been called Thoph ever since he, or anyone else, could remember—met them at the barn door. Thoph was Grandpa Day's hired man. He had worked for the Day's ever since he left the "downstairs" school, which is now called the primary. He was as much a part of the establishment as Aurelia Higgins, the hired "girl," and Aurelia had been in the Day kitchen since long before Rogers and Dave were born. She was queen of that kitchen now, just as Thoph was boss of the barn. Their authority was recognized, acknowledged, and, you may be sure, frequently asserted. They were members of the family and important members, too.

Thoph grunted acknowledgement of the boys' greeting, glanced at the overflowing clothesbasket and admitted that they had done pretty well, considering.

"Considerin' who you be, I mean," he added. "I told Mrs. 'Lije she was takin' a chance when she sent you two off to the woods alone, without somebody to make you stick to your job. 'They'll get to skylarkin' and raisin' hob,' I told her, 'and the last thing they'll think about is scrabblin' hog cranberry.'

Humph, you must have done some scrabblin' though, or the greens was almighty plenty, one or t'other. Got the horse all het up, though. I expected it. Been gallopin' him, ain't ye? Didn't I tell you not to?"

Rogers laughed. "Old Major wouldn't gallop if you built a fire under him," he retorted. "Have to yell 'oats' in his starboard ear before you can get him to wake up and walk. Come on into the house, Dave. I'm three-quarters ice and the rest jelly. Gosh, it's cold!"

He headed for the kitchen. Dave lingered a moment. "Rog says you said it was going to snow, Thoph," he asserted. "Think 'twill, do you?"

Thoph scratched his chin, an operation which sounded like rubbing a file across sandpaper. "If it don't, I don't know signs when I see 'em. Been smurrin' up over to the west'ard all mornin' and now it's thicker'n burgoo and black as a nigger's pocket all acrost yonder. Yes, sir, it'll snow—and blow, too, or I'm away off the course. Better rub some of your grandmarm's Arabian Balsam on your back afore you turn in. You and Rog'll need to be limber to tackle them shovels tomorrow.... Humph!" he added. "I'm hopin' it won't set in too thick afore the down coach gets along. Your Cousin Fred and his girl are comin' on that, you know."

"Um-hm, I know. Say, Thoph, do you think there's

any chance of Pa and Ma getting home by Christmas Day?"

"Not much, unless they've made port since last news we had, and that was day afore yesterday. Been due in Boston any day for over a fortni't. Calms and head winds held 'em up, most likely. Still, you can't never sometimes tell. The *White Foam's* an able craft. She'll sail if anything will."

The house was beginning to look Christmasy already. The front parlor windows were open and so were the doors from that stately apartment to the front hall and the sitting-room, which meant "airing out." Through the open doors one might catch glimpses of the fireplace and mantel, the flowered carpet, the gilt-framed portraits on the wall, and the painting of "The Highlands of the Hudson" which hung over the melodeon. Grandma bought that masterpiece from the artist himself, who called at the house one day exhibiting and offering for sale specimens of his work. He had a dozen other pictures, but Grandma selected this one because she thought it "so bright and cheerful." It was, too.

The boys did not linger to look at the front parlor. They saw it almost every Sunday, and in their minds it was associated with dress-up clothes and orders not to touch this or that. The sitting-room was far less grand but homey and comfortable. Sofas and chairs that were meant to sit upon, not just to look at, and the paintings on its walls were almost all of ships or barks which Grandpa had commanded at one time or other. There was one of the *White Foam*. Captain Edgar—Father, that was—had that picture painted when he was on the voyage before this one—Mother had not been with him then—and it showed the *White Foam* entering the port of Surinam, which was, of course, in South America. A real South American had painted it, and each rope and spar was exactly where it should be and the wave crests were as regularly spaced as fence pickets.

David hurried through the sitting-room—he had been careful to wipe his feet before entering the house by the side door, the one under the lattice porch where the wisteria bloomed in summer—and, having hung his heavy reefer jacket and tippet and cap on the folding hatrack in the entry, went out to the little "back room" between the dining-room and kitchen. The pump and sink were there—not the kitchen pump and sink, of course, but the others— and found Rogers already there, washing up. The kitchen door was open and the smell of those Christmas cookies was stronger and more enticing than ever. Grandma, capped and aproned, came in to ask if they had brought the evergreens. She better bet they had, slathers of 'em. Thoph would be bringing in the clothesbasket, solid brimming full, any minute.

Grandma said they were good boys and ordered Aurelia to give them each a cooky. Dave accepted his eagerly and devoured it forthwith. Rogers, as became his advanced years, was less effusively grateful, but ate the cooky nevertheless. He told Aurelia that, so far as he could judge by the sample, she had done pretty well. Could tell better, of course, if he had another one.

David giggled at his brother's audacity and giggled again when Aurelia, after calling them a pair of "young pigs," gave them each a second sample. The boys went up to their room, on the second floor, at the rear, to change and "fix up" before the company came. Dave's hair dressing was little more than a quick combing and a "slick up" with the brush, but Rogers was more painstaking.

"I know what ails you," declared his brother. "You're making so much fuss over yourself just 'cause that Emily's coming. You're girl-struck! Ho, ho!"

Rogers twisted his forelock into a becoming wave across his forehead. "Run away and play with your top, little boy," he ordered loftily. "Keep your nose clean and say 'Yes, ma'am' when she speaks to you."

"I will not!" cried David indignantly. "She *isn't* any older than I am, same as I told you. Anybody'd think I'd never seen a girl before, to hear you talk."

"Don't bother me, child. There"—regarding his reflection in the mirror with distinct approval—"that ought to make 'em look twice, eh? Cap'n Rogers H. Day, commander of the clipper *Queen of the Seas.* Sounds good, don't you think? Better get used to it, 'cause that's what it'll be one of these fine days.... Eh? What is it?"

Dave was looking out of the window. Over the leafless top of the pear tree in the yard he could catch a glimpse of the road, where it curved over the rise beyond Captain Seth Haven's house.

"I saw— Yes; look, isn't that the coach coming now?"

Rogers sprang to his side, pushed him out of the way, and peered from the window. The next moment he was running to the head of the stairs. David followed, but far more leisurely. If it was the stagecoach he had seen—and Rog wouldn't have galloped off like that if it had not been—it was bringing Cousin Fred and Emily. Cousin Fred was all right, citified and— oh, sort of grand and all that—but always good-natured. He wasn't afraid of Cousin Fred. He tried to tell himself that he wasn't afraid of Emily, either. Why should he be? Last time he had seen her—that was five years and more ago, of course—she was just a little girl, like other little girls. They had played "keep house" together and stuff like that. She would

have liked to play with dolls, but he drew the line
—except when one of the dolls was sick and he was the
doctor, that was sort of fun. But now—why, Rog
said she was grown up. Bosh! Course she wasn't. As
to her being prettier than Susie Taylor—why, that
must be more bosh! When Susie Taylor looked at
you over her shoulder and sort of half smiled, it—it
made a fellow feel—

David couldn't have told you exactly how it made
a fellow feel, and untold millions would not have
made him openly admit any feeling except masculine
superiority. But, as he went slowly down the stairs
and along the hall to the front door, he was uneasily
conscious that there was something odd somewhere.
Oh, what set Rog to talking all that junk for? Girls!
Aw, who gave a darn, anyway?

By the time he reached the front gate the stagecoach was in plain sight. Four horses, trotting smartly.
Eben Tidditt—Thoph's third cousin, he was—on the
driver's seat. Eben's cap was canted carefully to port
at just the right angle, the reins were looped in his
left hand, the whip was in his right, and he rocked
easily with the motion of the vehicle. Eben was en-
joying his job. Not as fine a job as commanding a
square-rigger, but as near to it as anything on land
could be.

Grandpa and Grandma and Aurelia came hurrying from the front door of the house; the fact that they used the front door proved the importance of the occasion. Thoph came running from the yard. Eben jerked the reins and bellowed "Whoa!" The stagecoach pulled alongside the Day front gate and stopped. Eben tucked the reins between the whip-socket and the dash, deliberately clambered from his throne, and opened the coach door.

A tall man, spare, dark-whiskered, beaver-hatted, alighted first. Cousin Fred Haynes, that was. David, hanging back a bit as the others of the welcoming group pushed forward, looked him over. Not for long, however; for then, from the coach emerged— the paragon.

She *had* grown up, Rog was right in that. Not that she was tall; in fact, she was not quite as tall as David himself. Prettier than Susie Taylor? Well, why, perhaps so and perhaps not. But different—oh, yes, there was no doubt of that. He could not have analyzed the difference. It was there, that is all he knew. From the little hat, with the yellow curls beneath it, the fur-trimmed cape and tightly buttoned little jacket, the white fur mittens, the skirt with the white stockings and trim bootees below it—she was different. And it wasn't just her clothes, either. As he remembered her she was just a girl, nice enough as girls went, which was not very far. Now—

David looked, gulped, and the portrait of Susie Taylor fell from the wall of his mind and shivered to bits. He, too, had been growing up.

Cousin Fred shook hands with Grandpa and Aurelia and Thoph and kissed Grandma. Grandpa and Grandma hugged and kissed Emily. Rogers and Emily shook hands. Even the blasé Rog was a trifle flustered, but she did not seem to be. And now Grandma was leading him, David, to the front.

"Davie, this is Emily. You remember her, course you do. Emmie, this is Davie. You haven't seen him for ever so long. My, how you've both grown since then! Doesn't seem possible, hardly."

Dave was conscious that a white fur mitten was extended in his direction. As he took it in his own red, briar-scratched paw he was also conscious that the nails of that paw were not quite so immaculate as he had thought them. He wished Grandma wouldn't call him Davie before folks; it sounded so—so kiddy. He blushed and grinned. Emily smiled. She said, "How do you do, Cousin David?" David responded with an embarrassed "hello." Then Grandpa shooed them all into the house.

He did not see her again until she had removed her hat and cape and mittens. Then he noticed that the rest of her hair was as yellow as the sample which had shown beneath the hat and that her eyes were a—

33

a kind of blue. Not that those details made any difference, so far as the general effect upon him was concerned. David Day was suffering from the shock of his first attack of love-sickness. Calf love, certainly, but all the more devastating and bewildering on that account.

Cousin Fred and Grandma and Grandpa went into the sitting-room to talk. Grandma said: "Now, Rogers, you and Davie must take Emmie in charge and see that she has a real good time. Perhaps she would like to see the barn and the horses and the pigs and hens and ducks and everything."

Rogers took charge of the expedition—he would, of course. He took charge of Emily, too. She and he walked together, and Dave tagged along behind. They visited the barn, the carriage-house and harness-room, which smelled of leather, and the stable, which smelled of hay and horse. They leaned over the wooden fence and looked down at the pig. There had been three pigs, but there was only one now, the others having gone to the smoke-house and the pickling barrels. They inspected the hens and the ducks. They even called on the cow, and Emily patted the white spot on her forehead and said she was a "nice old thing." David realized, for the first time, that being just a cow had some compensations.

They talked with Thoph. Rogers, completely recovered from whatever embarrassment he may have felt, was the leader in the conversation. Rogers was "showing off" a little bit. **U. S.** 726550

"Hey, Thoph," crowed Rog, "where's all that snow you said we were going to have? We haven't seen any yet. Better hurry it up. Emmie and I want to go sleigh riding."

Thoph grunted. "Cal'late you ain't looked out door for the last five minutes or so," he observed. "Might pay you to look now, smart boy."

Emily laughed when he called Rogers smart boy. David wanted to laugh, too, but he thought perhaps he had better not. They went to the door of the barn. Sure enough, snow was falling; not a great deal of it, but some.

"Just beginnin' to spit now," said Thoph, "but there's plenty up aloft. Hear that wind a-whinin'? There'll be plenty of that, too."

By five o'clock it was snowing heavily, and the wind was wailing and whistling about the gables and eaves of the house. The boys heard it when they were in the big bed in their room, with the patchwork quilts and comforters piled upon them. Rogers was inclined to be talkative after the lamp was out, but David had little to say.

"Well," crowed Rogers, "what do you think of Cousin Emmie now? Prettier than any girl in this town, isn't she? *And* different, eh?"

David did not attempt to deny it. "She isn't really our cousin though," he declared. "Cousin Fred isn't her father at all. He was her ma's second husband, and Emmie was born before she married Cousin Fred. That makes her no relation to us."

"Huh! How did you know so much? Grandma told you, I suppose likely?"

"No, she never. Emmie told me herself, this afternoon when you'd gone upstairs to brush your hair again. You're getting awful fussy, seems to me. Primping yourself up twice in one day."

"Never you mind that. Whew! hear that snow slat against the window. Let it come, I say. Grandpa said that, if it snowed enough and the roads were cleared, I could have Major and the sleigh tomorrow, maybe. Emmie's crazy about sleighing, she said so."

David was silent. He did not ask if he might go on the sleigh ride. He knew better. Two years more, though, and he would be as old as Rogers was now. Yes, and Emily would still be just his age. That was a comforting thought.

3

ALL THAT NIGHT and most of the next day the wind blew and the snow fell and drifted. It was not until mid-afternoon that the slaty sky reddened slightly in the west and the flakes became more scattered and, at last, ceased to descend. Thoph, condescendingly triumphant because of the fulfillment of his weather prophecy, appeared at the back door, booted, earlapped, mittened and tippeted, a shovel in his hands.

"Tumble out, all hands," he ordered. "Where are them two roustabouts of mine? 'Relia, you tell 'em it's time to stop loafin' below decks and report. I'll give 'em somethin' to make 'em forgit their growin' pains."

The boys were in the sitting-room, with Emily, playing parchesi. Parchesi was an interesting game and perfectly moral, not like playing with regular cards. Grandpa and Grandma played euchre sometimes, when Captain and Mrs. Bacon came for the evening; but cards for young people were taboo in that house. Rogers had not been lucky at parchesi that afternoon, Emily and David having won most of the games, so he hailed Aurelia and her message with a shout. He jumped to his feet, upsetting the

37

board. The dice box and the dice and markers fell to the floor and rolled every-which-way.

Emily protested. "You've spilled everything," she said.

"Never mind. Dave'll pick 'em up, he always does. Be lively about it, too, young-one; don't dawdle around. You've got work to do, and I'm going to see that you do it. Want to come and watch me shovel, Emmie? Come ahead. It's better than being boxed up in here, playing kids' games."

He hurried to the entry for his outdoor garments. Emily started to follow, but hesitated, turned back and knelt on the floor beside David, who was reaching under the sofa, collecting the scattered dice.

"Let me help you," she said. "There's one, way over there. I'll get it."

"No, you needn't. I can reach it easier than you can. You go along with Rog; don't you want to?"

"I don't know. Do you always do everything he tells you to?"

"Eh? No, not always. 'Most always, I suppose."

"Why?"

"Oh—just because, I guess. He's older than I am."

"Not such an awful lot. What makes you let him order you around? I wouldn't."

"Wouldn't you?"

"Course I wouldn't." Then, with a toss of the head, "Just let him try it and you'll see."

David was conscious of a thrill, but all he could think of to say was "Gee!" so he said that.

Emily picked up the last of the markers and restored it to the box.

"I don't like him to boss you so much," she declared. "Next time he does it I'm going to tell him not to."

Dave's thrill extended to his toes, but all he said was, "Aw, it's nothing. I don't mind. Come on, let's go."

The shoveling lasted until dark, and even then was but partially completed. Thoph shoveled and superintended. Rogers labored strenuously; Emily was watching and he couldn't resist showing off a little. David did his best to keep up, the perspiration running from beneath his cap brim. Even Grandpa and Cousin Fred came out and took a hand for a time.

"Do you good, Fred," said Grandpa with a chuckle. "Take some of the stiffness out of that ramrod, citified back of yours."

Cousin Fred laughed, but changed the laugh to a stifled groan. His shoveling did not amount to much.

The young people went to bed early; they were tired, even if they did not admit it. There was no hanging of stockings. Stocking hanging was by no means a universal custom in Bayport in the early fifties, and, in the few families where it was encouraged, only the younger children did it. Christmas trees were unknown, and the giving of Christmas gifts not yet what it had become even then in some other sections.

The morning broke clear, crisp and almost windless. A glorious Christmas Day. From the windows the landscape was white, with patches of green where the pine boughs showed beneath their load of snow. That stretch of blue and silver was the sea sparkling in the sunshine. Everyone came downstairs early. The rooms were gay with the wreaths and festoons. Grandpa was dressed in his Sunday suit, blue coat, shiny shoes and black satin stock, with the sharp collar points showing above it. Grandma had on her best black silk with lace at the collar and wrists, her best lace cap, her jet earrings and jet and diamond breastpin. Aurelia wore her black alpaca and her starched apron with the ruffles. She had her "extra hair" on, too. Even Thoph was dressed up, and his red face glistened where the dull razor had polished it.

A big breakfast, a Christmas breakfast: hot rye muffins, eggs, fried salt mackerel and fried potatoes, pancakes, cookies, doughnuts—even pie, if you wanted it.

The "town gang," men and youths with plows and scrapers and shovels, were digging out the road. They reported snow and heavy going everywhere. "No stagecoach through far as this today," they said. "It was doubtful if the steam cars," meaning the train from Boston, "had got through to Sandwich." The train was even yet something of a novelty on the Cape. Not so many years since travelers had to make the entire journey by stage. And now they were preparing the way for the railway's extension to Yarmouth. Captain Elijah prophesied that his grandchildren would live to see the day when a person could start from Boston in the morning and get to Provincetown before night—yes, even sooner than that. And not travel by sailing packet, either.

The road-clearing crew were a good-natured lot. They shouted "Merry Christmas" to the folks along the way. Rogers and Dave and Emily shouted it back at them. The trio were in high spirits. They had received their presents when they came down to breakfast. Grandpa had given each of the boys a jackknife and fifty cents to spend as he pleased. Grandma gave them new pairs of mittens and socks which she herself had knitted. Aurelia's present to each was a new kind of earlaps—"ear muffs," she called them. They were like pockets for your ears to fit into, warmly padded, and kept in place by an elastic under the chin. They put them on and decided that, although they looked kind of funny, they felt first-rate. Emily wanted to try them on, and they looked funny on her, too.

"I wouldn't wear them at home in Boston for anything," she confessed, "but I should think they would be real nice down here."

Rogers laughed. "*I* shan't wear 'em much," he proclaimed. "I'm not going to be around here much longer, anyhow. I'd look pretty coming on deck of a ship with my ears tucked to bed in those things, wouldn't I? Ho, ho! You can have mine for a spare pair, after I've gone to sea, Dave. All right for land-lubbers like you, boy."

Emily's gift from her stepfather was a cameo pin, a tiny bunch of flowers carved in coral in the middle, with a real gold frame surrounding it. The boys gazed at it in awe; it was almost as fine as Grandma's jet and diamond one and must have cost lots of money. Grandma gave Emily a handkerchief with her name worked in blue silk at one corner and a pretty pair of hair ribbons. She was wearing the ribbons, one at each side of her face, and against the rosy flush of her cheeks they were very becoming. Rogers said they were. Dave would have liked to say so, too, but he was afraid it might sound silly, coming from him.

At eleven Cousin Bailey and Cousin Becky and Jeddie arrived. Cousin Bailey's last name was Howes. Cousin Becky was his wife, and twelve-year-old Jeddie was their son. They lived at Denboro, the next village up the Cape from Bayport. They came in a sleigh, and on the way down they had stopped at West Bayport for Aunt Desire and brought her with them. Aunt Desire's last name was Snow, and she was Martha Day's sister-in-law. Her husband had gone down with the brig *Flora* in a gale off Hatteras. Aunt Desire, therefore, was a widow and never permitted people to forget the fact. Captain Judah Snow had been dead six years, but Aunt Desire's caps were still edged with black and her handkerchiefs had black borders. In the estimation of her nephews she, as an adjunct to a merry Christmas, rated ten below zero.

Cousin Bailey reported plenty of snow and rough traveling. The sleigh, he said, had rocked all the way like a dory in the Monomoy tide rips. "Made me think of old times fishing off the Banks in February," he declared. "Didn't know but Desire would be seasick, but she weathered it without shifting cargo. Eh, Desire?"

Aunt Desire groaned. "Such a cruise *I* never had," she declared. " 'Livia, do you suppose I could have a cup of hot ginger tea? No, no, not real tea. That always goes right straight to my nerves, but ginger

45

tea seems to sort of soothe them. Sure 'twon't be *too* much trouble? Thank you ever so much. I know my foot is wet. One of my galoshes leaks like a sieve, and I went in up to—well, over my ankles—getting out to that pesky sleigh."

Cousin Bailey's first inquiry was whether or not anything had been heard from Edgar and Martha. Grandpa said no. The *White Foam's* arrival in Boston had not been reported when he last heard from there.

Cousin Jeddie—his dressed-up name was Jedediah —was turned over to the juvenile group, who welcomed him with but tepid enthusiasm. Jeddie was freckled, decidedly plump—not to say fat—for his age, and intellectually anything but a ball of fire. Rogers and David and Emily dutifully conducted him about the estate, and the only spot which seemed to interest him was the pigpen. Even then he remarked that he didn't think much of *that* hog. "You ought to see the one we've got. Make two of that runt, he would."

His interest awoke, however, when Aurelia called them in to dinner. He was the first of the quartette in the dining-room. The table was a sight to see. The best china—from China it was, too; the silver teapot and hot water jug given Grandpa by the owners of the bark *Caroline* after he had taken her captain, crew and two passengers aboard his own ship in mid-ocean, the *Caroline* being on fire at the time; the silver spoons, funny little things with fiddle backs, which were Grandma's grandmother's wedding present and had been handed down in the family; the Waterford glass flower holder, another heirloom; the tablecloth and napkins which Father had bought in London when he was there on his first voyage as captain and brought home to the old folks; the—oh, well, about everything that was hidden away most of the time and brought out and used only on special occasions like this one.

Grandpa sat at one end of the table, of course, and Grandma at the other. Cousin Fred and Cousin Bailey and Cousin Becky and Aunt Desire were scattered along at judicious intervals, with the three boys and Emily each next to a grown-up. Aurelia and Obed Pratt's oldest girl Hettie—she had been hired for the day to help "wait"—were in the kitchen ready to serve when Grandma rang the little silver bell with the carved ivory handle. It came from Calcutta, that bell; Uncle Isaac, the one who was lost at sea, brought it home from there himself.

Grandpa looked about the table. So did Grandma. The hum of conversation ceased. Heads were bowed. Grandpa cleared his throat, bowed his own head, and said grace. It was the same grace he always said; David and Rogers knew every word of it by heart.

Its principal merit, to their minds, was that it wasn't very long. The Reverend Mr. Seymour, minister of the old First Meeting House, sometimes wasted almost ten minutes when he was a guest at that table.

When the amen came, Grandma rang the bell and Aurelia came in with the turkey. A regular man's size turkey, too; weighed nigh to sixteen pounds, according to Thoph's estimate. She set the overflowing platter in front of Grandpa. Then Hettie brought in a mammoth chicken pie and set it before Grandma at the other end of the table. You could have turkey or chicken pie, just as you pleased, or both. Almost everybody took both. Aunt Desire said Christmas was such a sad day for her; it had always meant so much to poor dear departed Judah. Judah was her husband's name. She said she didn't feel as if she could bear to eat one single thing. She did though, and bore it remarkably well.

Then came the vegetables: potatoes and squash and turnips and onions; two big dishes of cranberry sauce and a smaller one of crab-apple jelly; and hot biscuits, mounds of them. There was cider, big pitchers of it. Grandpa lifted his goblet.

"Just a minute, all hands," he ordered. "Before we start in, let's drink to those we hoped to have with us today. They're full as disappointed as we are, you can be sure of that. We'll wish 'em a Merry Christ-

48

mas now and hope they'll be here in time to wish us a Happy New Year. Edgar and Martha, God bless 'em!"

They all drank, youngsters and all. Intoxicants were forbidden to minors in that household, but cider was just cider, so it was all right. Grandma's eyes were damp as she sipped hers. She had so looked forward to her son's and daughter's return in time for that dinner. David did not dare look at his brother; he was not certain of the condition of his own eyes. Ma and Pa! Godfreys, if they only *were* here! He swallowed, saw Emily glancing in his direction, and tried hard to grin.

Between courses—that is, before the plum pudding and mince pie and nuts and raisins and apples were brought in—the youngsters went out in the yard to run about a little and, as Jeddie said, "Shake down what we've et and make room for some more." To run three times around the house was the regular custom, but the snow was too deep for that, so they trotted up and down in the shoveled driveway. They were about to go in again—it was chilly and damp in the yard—when Dave, who was nearest the entrance of the drive, called to them to wait a minute.

"Somebody's coming," he shouted. "I hear sleigh-bells."

Rogers said: "What of it? There'll be lots of sleigh-

49

ing now that the road is getting cleared. Come on, boy, come on!"

"Hurry up!" urged Jeddie. "Ain't you hungry? I am."

But Dave, for some reason which he could not have defined or explained, lingered. The sleigh was coming from the westward. He could see it now, turning the bend beyond Captain Haven's. Three people in it, the driver on the front seat and a man and a woman—at least he guessed one was a woman, they were so muffled up he could scarcely tell—on the seat behind. The horse was a stranger to him. Bayport boys knew every horse in town by sight, just as they knew every person, and David had never before seen this animal.

He stepped out into the road, where he could see more clearly above the heaped snow at its sides. The people in the sleigh could see him now. The driver in the sleigh turned his head and spoke to the pair behind him, and one of the pair—the man—stood up in the sleigh, waved and shouted.

David's heart stopped beating for an instant, or he felt as if it did. His breath caught in his throat, choking him. Then it burst forth in a hysterical shriek. "Pa! ... Ma! ... Oh! ... Oh!" he screamed and ran headlong. The sleigh drew up beside the Day gate. Its passengers did not wait for their driver to assist

50

them to the ground; they cast off robes and wraps and sprang out by themselves.

The next moment David's head was pressed close to the breast of his mother's cloak, her arms were holding him tight, and his father's hand was patting his shoulder. More than a year since he had felt that hug or the touch of that hand. He—he— Oh, what was the matter with him? Rogers would be there in a second, and he mustn't catch him crying. Certainly there was nothing to *cry* about. But then, Mother was crying, too.

4

THAT was a Christmas! As long as they lived the two boys would remember it. The triumphant progress to the house. Father and Mother and Rogers and Dave in a tumultuous, joyous huddle, and Emily, open-eyed and excited, with Jeddie, open-mouthed and awe-stricken, forming the rear guard. Grandpa and Grandma and Cousin Fred and Cousin Becky and Cousin Bailey and Aunt Desire meeting them at the door. Aurelia and Thoph—Thoph had been eating his Christmas dinner in the kitchen with Aurelia and Hettie—coming into the dining-room to shake hands and welcome the wanderers home. Thoph declared that he had never given them up.

"All hands kept tellin' me you'd never make it for Christmas, Cap'n Edgar," he crowed, "but I wouldn't harken to 'em. I says to Davie, here, I says: 'You can't most always sometimes tell.' Them's the very words I said, wan't they, Dave? He didn't pay much attention to me, but—"

Aurelia broke in. "Oh, be still!" she commanded. "Can't you wait till folks have done dinner before you start up your windmill? Land sakes above, I don't suppose Cap'n Edgar nor Mrs. Marthy have had anything to eat since I don't know when. There's plenty of everything left, though. You two set right down and I'll fetch it in."

She pushed the still orating Theophilus out of the dining-room. Captain Edgar called after her to ask her to look out for the driver of the sleigh.

"He hasn't had any dinner, either," he added, "and if it hadn't been for him Martha and I wouldn't be here now. He drove us all the way from Barnstable, and I rather guess ours was the first sleigh since the storm to get through from as far as that. Load him to the hatches, 'Relia."

So the dinner began all over again. That is, the others waited in their places at the table while Captain Edgar and his wife "caught up." There was more talking than eating, of course. The *White Foam* had got in to Boston two days before. Captain and Mrs. Day had taken the train the following noon and, although it was snowing heavily, reached Sandwich eventually, but hours late. Progress beyond that point, however, was out of the question. Roads were blocked and trees blown down. They put up at the Sandwich tavern and remained there until early morning of the present day—Christmas. Then Captain Edgar routed out an adventurous soul, who, for a price, agreed to try to get them as far as Barnstable "if the horse and sleigh stayed together."

"That was a ride, eh, Martha?" observed the captain. "Of course, *I* never would have risked it, but you," with a wink at his wife, "just wouldn't be put off."

"Nonsense!" protested Martha. "You were the one who declared you were going to get home Christmas Day in spite of—ahem—something and high water. Lucky I am used to rough voyages, though."

They reached Barnstable, safe and whole, and there was another delay while the captain negotiated with another livery-stable keeper for transportation to Bayport. That was, at last, arranged and they came on.

"Cost you something, didn't it?" queried Grandpa Elijah, with a chuckle. His son nodded.

"Why, yes, now you mention it. But"—with a

wave of his hand and a glance about the table—"look what I got for my money."

The trunks—their contents included the presents brought from abroad—were still in storage at the Sandwich tavern, but no one, even the boys, cared about that. To the latter it was quite sufficient to have Pa and Ma home again, to hear Pa call them his first and second mates and have Ma look and look at them and smile that—oh, sort of—you know—comforting smile of hers. There would be long talks by and by, when no one else was around. She would want to know about everything. So would Pa, but, in some ways, and about some things, he was easier to talk to. In others, though, not nearly so easy. Pa sometimes laughed in the wrong place, but Ma—well, she would understand and would not laugh.

Games that evening in the sitting-room. Everyone, Grandpa and Grandma included, took part in them. They played "Kitchen Furniture," that game where names of all sorts of kitchen things like "Frying Pan" or "Rolling Pin" or "Teakettle" are written on slips of paper and put in a hat. You draw one and then that is your name, although you mustn't tell anyone else. You mustn't forget it either, because, by and by, when all the players but one are sitting in a sort of circle, the other one in the middle—the one who is It and is blindfolded—will turn around quick and point and, if you are the one pointed at, you must jump up and say your name three times. If the It one can count ten before you remember and say the name the three times, you have to be It yourself.

It was fun. Even Rogers, who was, as a general rule, contemptuously superior to this sort of thing, had to laugh when dignified Cousin Fred, taken unawares, jumped up and shouted "Skittle—Skittle—Skittle" instead of Skillet, which was what he ought to have said. And all Aunt Desire ever said when they pointed at her, was: "Eh? What? Is it me? Oh, my soul!" and stuff like that. Aunt Desire would have been It all the time if the others had not taken pity on her.

At ten the juveniles were ordered to bed. Jeddie had eaten so much that he was half asleep already. David had heard Rogers go upstairs ahead of him, but when he reached their bedroom he was surprised to find that his brother was not there. He stepped out into the upper hall to see what had become of him.

There was no sign of Rogers, but Emily was on her way to her room at the front of the house—she and her father had the best spare room and the little room next it—and she and David met. David, whose conscience was, for a certain reason, troubling him a little, mumbled good night and would have passed her by, but she detained him.

"Oh, Dave," she whispered.

"Eh? Yes?"

"Don't talk loud, I don't want anybody else to hear. Where's Rogers?"

"Don't know. Thought he came up ahead of me, but I guess he didn't. Why? Want to see him?"

"No, I wanted to see you. Papa and I are going tomorrow morning, did you know it?"

"Um-hm."

"Are you sorry?"

"Eh? Guess so. Yes, I am."

"I'm sorry, too—I've had a lovely time. . . . Dave."

"Yes?"

"I—I've lost something that belongs to me. I think I lost it this morning, when we were outside, all of us, after Jeddie came and before we went in to dinner. Do you know what it was?"

David flushed. "I—I—" he faltered.

"It was one of the hair ribbons Grandma gave me. You picked it up, didn't you?"

David gulped. "Um-hm," he admitted, wretchedly.

"I saw you pick it up. Why didn't you give it to me?"

"I—I don't know." That was the truth, he did not know exactly why he had kept the ribbon. He had not meant to. And it had burned a hole in his conscience ever since.

"I—I'd have given it to you if you'd asked me," he mutttered. "Here it is."

He took the crumpled ribbon from his pocket and held it out in her direction. He did not look at her, however.

"I—I'm awful sorry, Em. G'night."

He was turning away, but she spoke his name.

"Dave."

"Yes? Oh, what is it?" he cried desperately. "I said I was sorry. You can tell 'em if you want to."

"I don't want to. I shan't ever tell anybody. David, did you keep the ribbon because—because it was mine?"

There was no answer at all this time. Emily waited but an instant.

"Dave."

"Yes—oh, *yes*. Aw, please, Emmie—"

"Dave, I knew you had it and I didn't care. Truly I didn't. Would you—would you like to have it? If I gave it to you? To keep, I mean? Because if you would—well, you can. Good night."

She was hurrying down the hall. He gazed at the ribbon in his hand. Then a disturbing thought came crashing into the whirligig of his mind. He ran after her.

"Emmie," he whispered. "Tell me! Did—did you give Rog anything to—to keep—same as this?"

"No. Course I didn't."

"Are you going to?"

"No," indignantly. "Why should I?"

"Godfreys! But—but why did you give it to me?"

"Because I think you're nice. I like you, that's why. Good night."

"Godfreys! Er—er— Thanks, Em."

David had been in bed almost an hour when Rogers came tiptoeing into the room. He closed the door carefully and then, to his brother's astonishment, began to perform a wild, but silent, war dance on the braided rug.

"What's the matter with you?" demanded David. "What you acting like that for?"

Rogers concluded the war dance with one final pirouette. He came over to the bed.

"Boy," he chortled vaingloriously, "you know what you're looking at, do you? You're looking at a sailor, that's what. I'm going to sea. Yes sir-ee, I am, and I'm going before the month's out, too. Hooray for our side! Whoop! *Whe-ee!*"

He had hidden in the hall closet instead of coming up to bed and then, after a precautionary interval, had listened at the crack of the sitting-room door.

"Cousin Bailey and Cousin Becky and Aunt Desire

and Ma and Grandma had gone aloft to turn in," he confided, "but Pa and Grandpa and Cousin Fred hadn't. They stayed down to smoke and talk, and I was almost sure they were going to talk about me. Cousin Fred is going tomorrow, and I figured this would be their only chance away from the women-folks. And they did talk about me, too. Cousin Fred is going to get me that berth as cabin boy on that Leghorn voyage under Cap'n Seabury. Pa's agreed to let me go, too. Oh, *gosh!*"

It was after midnight when the pair were suffi-ciently composed to sleep. Rogers' final remark was a rainbowed prophecy.

"Cabin boy this year. Second mate next year. First mate pretty soon after that, and then Cap'n. Cap'n Rogers H. Day, commander of the clipper so and so! Whew! *I'll* make some of these old-time slow-poke skippers sit up, just watch me. And then—well, Cousin Fred and I will be seeing a lot of each other, and Emily and I will see a lot of each other and— Say, didn't I tell you she was a great girl! It takes your Uncle Rog to pick the good ones, eh? *Has* this been a Merry Christmas? Oh, gosh!"

David did not answer. He was a trifle envious of his brother's good luck, but not as envious as he might have been had it not been for his meeting with Emily in the upper hall. Rogers might be able to, as he said,

61

"pick the good ones," but it looked as if the good ones did not always pick Rogers. There was that blue hair ribbon carefully tucked away under David's small pile of handkerchiefs in the bureau drawer.

Yes, it *had* been a Merry Christmas.

PART TWO

The Sixties

PART TWO: THE SIXTIES

I

Bᴜᴛ do you think you are strong enough, Davie?" asked Grandma. She still called him Davie, although he was twenty-three years old and taller by a head than she was herself. Age nor height nor the fact that he had won his rank as captain of a full-rigged ship when he was twenty-one made any difference to Grandma. To her he was still Davie and would be as long as she lived.

Captain Edgar answered for his son.

"Course he is, Mother," he said. "It's a fine day and the walk will do him good. Feel all right, don't you, Dave?"

"Fit as a fiddle, Father. High time I stretched my legs. You and Mother and Grandma and Emmie come along in the carryall when Thoph has it ready for you, and I'll walk on ahead. I'll be at the church by the time you get there—or sooner."

Emily spoke then. "I'd like to walk myself," she said. "Wait for me at the gate; I'll be with you in a jiffy."

David put on his overcoat, took his hat from the rack by the side door and went out into the yard. As his father had said, it was a fine day. For the time of year, late December, a glorious day. There was a crisp tang in the air and, unusual for Bayport in winter, scarcely a trace of dampness.

David Day drew a long breath, filling his lungs to capacity. It was certainly good to get out of doors again. He had, of course, been out several times since they brought him home from the Washington hospital, but on those occasions he had been tucked up on the back seat of the carryall. It was a joy to be once more on his own, to step firmly, to feel the frozen ground crunch beneath his feet. Perhaps this really was the end of his long stretch in sick bay; he devoutly hoped so.

How long had it been, really? It seemed at least a century. Almost a year since he had informed his owners that he was giving up the merchant marine to become one of Uncle Sam's hired hands in the transport service. The owners did not reproach him; they understood how he felt and that the North welcomed every seaman of experience it could get. He could not hope for a captain's berth, of course—those went to the regular Navy men for the most part—but he did obtain a mate's appointment and spent six busy but disappointingly dull months on a craft carrying troops and supplies to and from South Atlantic ports. Not much fighting, few thrills or adventures of any kind. And then came the outbreak of typhoid fever, the weeks and weeks in hospital, the distressful journey home, and the long, discouraging convalescence. A grand career as a warrior, his!

He smiled, a trifle bitterly, as he thought of it. He would have been of quite as much use to his country and far more to himself if he had remained on the quarter-deck of his old ship. Rogers was doing that very thing. Rogers had strongly advised against his entering the transport service.

"What will you get out of it, Dave? Nothing. The pay doesn't amount to much and, unless you've got influence enough to wangle a job in the regular Navy after the war is over, you'll have lost a whale of a lot of time. You've done first rate so far; people are calling you a smart cap'n already. Keep on handling your own vessel and bossing your own crews. You won't have to touch your hat and say 'sir' to anybody, then. You can bet your sou'wester that's what I'm going to do. Somebody's got to keep the trade flag flying or we'll all go to the poorhouse."

That was Rogers' conviction, and he stuck to it. Not because he was a coward, for he was anything but that. He believed what he said, and there was truth in it. The American merchant marine was in a bad way. Confederate privateers and armed cruisers had played havoc with it; shipping firms, many of them, were in bankruptcy; others, more cautious than patriotic, had put their vessels under British registry; the proud fleet which had carried the Stars and Stripes to all ports of the world in the '40's and '50's was dwindling to a pitiful remnant. There was much to be said for the owners who still sent out their ships with their country's colors at the masthead; and something for the captains who took the risk of commanding these ships.

Bayport, a salt-seasoned town, recognized all this, and its citizens thought no less of Captain Rogers Day because he stuck to his job. David shared this feeling, in a way, but his make-up was different from his brother's; he was less practical perhaps, and possibly more sentimental. At any rate, he had made his decision, and now, as he stood by the gate awaiting Emily, he did not regret having made it. He had done his best for the cause, he had tried hard, and, as soon as he was strong enough, he intended to go back and keep on trying. Only—well, why couldn't it have been a shell-blown splinter or a bullet that put him temporarily out of commission? Typhoid fever! He could have picked that up in a Bayport barnyard.

Emily came out of the side door and walked briskly toward him. She was prettier then ever—that realization came to him every time he looked at her. Prettier and more wonderful, but still as sweet and gracious and unaffected—natural, he would have called it—as she had been that Christmas evening when she told him he might keep the hair ribbon Grandma had given her. Nine—no, ten—years ago, that was. There had been so many changes since then, but she had not changed, except to grow from girlhood to womanhood.

"What are you thinking about?" she asked, as she came near.

"Eh? Oh, I don't know. Little of everything, I guess. Mainly what a lot of things can happen in ten years."

She nodded, sadly. "They can indeed," she agreed. "It was just ten years ago, wasn't it, when Father and I came down here for Christmas and Uncle Edgar and Aunt Martha arrived home from sea while we were eating Christmas dinner. Grandpa was alive then and Cousin Bailey and—and Father. We had such a wonderful time. I shall never forget that Christmas."

"Neither shall I."

Frederick Haynes had been dead more than a year now. And, when his estate was settled, people learned that, instead of being a wealthy man, he was almost a bankrupt. The war had ruined his business as it had that of so many others. His vessels had been wrecked, or burned by the Confederate cruisers; his Southern accounts had been cancelled; his notes could not be met; even the fine house on Beacon Street was heavily mortgaged. Emily had come to Bayport to live with Grandma Day. Captain Edgar and his wife—David and Rogers' mother and father—were living there, too. Captain Edgar had given up seafaring when Grandpa died.

David would have liked to say something serious and sympathetic, something to make her understand that he knew how she must be feeling at this Christmas season, but he did not. That had always been his trouble—lack of the right words at the right time. So, groping desperately, he said something entirely different.

"Do you remember how many times Jed passed his plate for turkey?" he asked. "I counted up to three and then 'twas time to pass my own, so I lost count."

She smiled. "Poor old Jeddie," she said. "I haven't seen him for ever so long."

"Nor I. But you needn't call him poor. Jed's in the fish business over at West Denboro. Owns shares in a couple of schooners and, from what I hear, is doing first-rate. Aunt Becky lives with him and bosses him around just as she did when he was ten. According to the yarn I heard he would like to get married, but his mother won't let him."

They walked on together along the main road. Many of the houses they passed were decorated, but not with Christmas greenery. Flags and strips of bunting were the decoration now. In the windows of Eldridge's General Store colored portraits of General Grant and Admiral Porter were displayed instead of the Christmas toys and novelties of a few years back. Buggies and carryalls filled with church-goers rattled by, and the sandy sidewalks were dotted with pedestrians. Bayport was a church-going community, and this was to be a combination patriotic and Christmas service.

The sheds by the First Meeting House were filled, and the overflow of horses and vehicles were parked about the grounds under the bare-limbed elms and silver-leafed poplars. On the platform by the church doors were groups shaking hands and exchanging greetings before entering. The men were wearing

73

their Sunday best and tall hats, and the skirts of the
women and girls spread and arched like giant mush-
rooms.

Friends and acquaintances came up to congratulate
David on his first appearance in public. Old Captain
Asaph Dilworthy declared he was glad to see him out
of dry dock. "That farm fever's an old Harry of a
disease," he declared. "Had it myself one time down
in Galveston. Wouldn't let me eat nothin' but milk
and everlastin' little of that. Got so that for a couple
of year afterwards I couldn't sight a cow without
gaggin'. They tell me Cap'n Rogers is expected home
time for Christmas. So, is it?"

David told him that Rogers' ship, the *Forward
Light*, was somewhere between Buenos Aires and
New York. They were hoping he might make a
quick voyage. Everybody, although they seemed glad
to see Dave, asked about Rogers. David heard Mrs.
Sophronia Hedge, widow of Captain Caleb Hedge,
talking with Emily.

"I hear Cap'n Rogers may be home 'most any time
now," she said. "Cap'n Edgar said he was waiting to
hear he'd made port. Nice if he got here before Christmas Day. How he would enjoy that! 'Twould be a
merry Christmas for him. And for others, too—especially *one*, eh, my dear? Oh, I know how you feel.
I can remember waiting for my husband when he was

on a home voyage and, my, how long the days seemed until he came!"

David did not hear Emily's reply. He did not wish to hear it. There had been no definite announcement

of her engagement to Rogers, but all Bayport took it as a settled and assured thing. Even Captain Edgar and his wife seemed to so regard it, although they did not talk about it.

Emily, herself, never mentioned it, to David nor, so far as he knew, to anyone else. Nevertheless he, too, took it for granted. Rogers always got what he

wanted. In conversations with his younger brother—
he was more confidential with the latter than with
others of the family, even his father and mother—
he made no secret of his ambitions. The ambitions
were many, but two were fixed and unalterable. The
first was to command a clipper ship; that he had already realized. The second was to marry Emily.

"Oh, I know she's got lots of fellows hanging
around," he said, "but they don't worry me. And
her father's got wads of money and I haven't any—
yet. But I will have some day and I'll have her, too.
She knows how I feel and she'll wait. Emily and I
understand each other."

It was said with all the assurance in the world, and
David believed it. Rogers was a wonderful fellow.
Rogers would be a great man and a rich man some
day. Rogers deserved all the good things that might
come his way. And Rogers was his brother. So, when
that brother boasted of an understanding between
Emily and himself, David manfully concealed his own
feelings, stamped into oblivion whatever faint hopes
he may have had, and offered congratulations. That
night, after hours of tossing wretchedness, he swore
an oath; he would not be jealous and he would be
loyal. Emily was worthy of the best in the world,
and who was better than Rogers? Certainly not he,
David Day. So that was that.

2

THE CHURCH was well-filled that morning. The
masculine heads above the backs of the pews
were, the majority of them, gray or black.
This was usually the case in the old First Meeting
House, for Bayport's young and middle-aged men,
most of them, were away at sea. Just now, however,
the war had taken some of the landlubbers. Zoeth
Havens, who used to clerk in the General Store, was
in the Army; so, too, was Frank Gale, the blacksmith's

helper; and Darius Doane, who used to drive Doctor Parker on his rounds. Ensign Luther Baker, in uniform, his arm in a sling, came up the aisle with his mother. Luther had been wounded in the operations before Charleston and was home on leave. The girls and young ladies turned to look admiringly at him as he passed. David, while he did not grudge Lute the admiration, did envy him the wound. At least it was proof that young Baker had been where fighting was going on. Whereas typhoid—oh, bah!

The service moved slowly. The choir sang its carefully rehearsed selection, the minister prayed for the President and the Generals and the Admirals and all who were risking their lives in their country's cause on land and sea, and preached a fervently patriotic sermon. Old Captain Winship fell asleep in the middle of it, as he generally did, and, when nudged by his wife's elbow, woke and audibly asked, "Eh? What's the matter, Susan?"

At last, after the benediction, the occupants of the Day pew—the same pew Captain Elijah had sat in, and his father before him, and his father's father before that—moved slowly out to the platform. Thoph was awaiting them with the carryall, and the family drove home together. Then they sat down to the dinner which Aurelia had cooked for them. Conversation during the meal was mainly about

Rogers. Everyone was disappointed at not having heard from him, and Grandma said she was afraid he wouldn't get here for Christmas, after all. Mother—Mrs. Captain Edgar—said she had not given up hope.

"Do you remember," she added, "how you and Father and everyone had given us up—Edgar and I, I mean—that Christmas after the big snowstorm? And *we* got here in time for dinner. How long ago was that? Let me see."

David answered the question. "Just ten years ago," he said. "I was thinking about it this morning. A grand Christmas, that was."

Emily put in a word. "I think it was the best Christmas I have ever had," she declared. "I remember telling Father so the next day, when we were on the train bound back to Boston. He said he had had a jolly time, too, and he hoped we would have a great many more like it."

The mention of Cousin Fred's name caused the talk to halt for an instant. Captain Edgar, after a quick glance at Emily, spoke.

"Christmas, when you come to think of it," he said, "has always been a lucky day for us Days. Things, and generally good things, seem to happen to us around this time. One of Father's pet yarns was about how, that time when you and he, Mother, were wrecked over in the Indian Ocean and had to take to the boats, the vessel that picked you up was sighted on Christmas morning. Best Christmas he ever had, he used to swear that was."

Grandma nodded. "It isn't likely I'll ever forget it," she vowed. Then, with a look about the dining-room: "It don't seem quite as Christmasy this year as it ought to be, somehow. No wreaths or hog cranberry vines around. We always used to have them when the boys were young and at home. Thoph said he would get some for me, but I guess likely we both forgot it."

After dinner Emily beckoned to David, and he followed her into the parlor.

"Dave," she said, "I have an idea. Let's you and I go up into the woods and get some Christmas greens. It will please Grandma and it will be fun, something to do, anyway. You know where to go, and Thoph will drive us there, I'm sure."

But Thoph was by no means as sure. He was hard at work whitewashing the inside walls of the carriage house. "Sort of slickin' the place up for Cap'n Rogers," he announced. "The Cap'n is always a great hand for havin' everything taut and shipshape, and when he fetches port I wouldn't want him to think the old man was gettin' sloppy in his old age."

It was Thoph's habit nowadays to refer to himself as an old man, but for any individual outside the family to call him that would have meant trouble. His once red hair was gray now, and his leathery jaws a trifle thinner, but he grimly declared himself able to "chew hay yet." There was no question of his ability to chew tobacco, and he was chewing it now.

"No, no, you won't neither," he vowed in answer to Dave's suggestion that they could do their own driving. "Fust place, I don't want you to, and second, I need the horse to do an errand with down to the store. Suppose I drive you up to the Pond and then

81

go and do my errand? Then I'll come up by and by, when I've got my whitewashin' done, and fetch ye both. How'll that set with ye?"

It would set very well indeed, and so it was done that way. He left them at the end of the wood road and rattled away in the two-seater. The sky had clouded over, and Sandy Pond looked as chilly and desolate as it had on the afternoon, ten years before, when the two Day boys came there, behind old Major, on the same errand. Now old Major was no more and the boys were men, but the evergreen and hog cranberry were showing just as profusely. Even the pitch pines and scrub oaks seemed to have grown but little.

David looked about him. "I like this place," he declared with emphasis. "I've had some good times up here; picnics and fishing in the summer and coming here in December to hunt Christmas greens, as we're doing now. Seems to belong to our Christmases—mine and Rogers'—if you know what I mean."

"Yes, I know. It looks as if it hadn't changed, and there have been so many changes. Even two years ago who would have thought I would be living here in Bayport, that it would be my home? I can scarcely believe it, even yet."

"Yes. Yes, that's so. I—well, I guess you know how we all feel, Emily. I don't know how to say it exactly, but—but we do understand, all of us. After the home you used to have our old-fashioned place down here in the country must seem pretty—well, second-rate."

He paused, not knowing exactly how to continue. She was not looking at him, so he made another attempt. "You've been mighty plucky through it all, Em," he added. "Not one complaint. Sometimes I wonder—"

She turned now and put out her hand in protest. "Don't! Please don't!" she begged.

"Eh? Don't? Have I—"

"No, no! You haven't done anything, or said anything, either, except— Only please don't talk in that way! You make me feel ashamed—almost wicked. Complaint! Why should I complain? If it hadn't been for you and Grandma and Uncle Edgar and Auntie, all of you, where should I be now? After Father died I was so *all* alone, or felt that I was. And then you dear people came and proved that I wasn't alone at all. You have taken me into your home and —oh, just made me feel that you really wanted me there. As if I belonged there. And I—truly I am beginning to—to hope I do belong. I love Bayport, and the old house. You mustn't call it second-rate; it is the dearest place in the world. I have always loved it,

ever since I first came here as a little bit of a girl. I—
Oh, *please* don't talk so! I—"

She choked and turned away once more. David
took an involuntary step toward her and then stepped
back again.

"I'm sorry, Emily," he faltered. "I guess I— You
see, I only meant—"

"Of course you did. And I didn't mean to say all
the things I did, although I have thought them often
enough. Well, we ought to be getting our evergreen,
hadn't we?"

He showed her where the evergreen was thickest
and how to separate the long streamers from the mat
of pine needles and dead leaves. He spread the carriage robe which Thoph had left with them on the
damp ground and they knelt side by side. Their
hands touched as they groped amid the vines. Dave
felt that he ought to talk, he must talk, but that the
things he wanted most to say were those that simply
must not be said. At last, however, he made a des-
perate attempt to say something.

"Well," he observed, trying to sound casual, "old
Rog will be home before long, won't he? And we
shall all be glad enough to see him. A great old boy,
Rogers is. He's having the luck of the family and
he deserves it. I don't grudge him a grain."

"No, I'm sure you don't. You wouldn't."

"Well, I don't. . . . And I won't."

His tone caused her to turn and look at him.

"Dave," she said.

"Eh? Yes?"

"You aren't very happy just now, are you?"

"What? Happy? Why—why, yes, guess I am. Why shouldn't I be?"

"I think I know why. It was awfully hard for you to give up your ship and go into the war, wasn't it? Oh, I know why you did it: you felt that you ought to, of course. And then—the fever and being sick so long, having to come home and stay—I understand. It isn't fair. It *isn't!*"

She reached over and laid a hand on his. "I'm so sorry," she said.

He caught his breath. Then after an instant: "That's all right," he muttered gruffly. "Didn't know I was playing cry-baby. No reason to find fault. Luck is luck, and mine may be better by and by. It's going to be; I'll make it."

"I know, but it isn't fair, just the same. Why should Rogers have all the good luck and you all the bad? He doesn't deserve it any more than you do, I don't care what you say. No," impulsively, "nor as much."

"Eh? Why, now, Emily, you mustn't talk that way. It isn't so, of course; and besides, you mustn't

85

say such things about Rogers—you, of all people."

"Why not me, of all people?"

"Because—well, considering—"

"Considering what?"

"Why—why, you and he are—are—well—oh, you know what I'm trying to say."

She rose to her feet. The color had risen to her cheeks and there was dangerous flash in her eyes.

"No," she retorted impatiently, "I don't know.... Well, yes, then, I suppose I do; but I am tired of hearing it, tired and sick of all the silly smiles and hints. When Mrs. Hedge was purring over me at church this morning I could hardly keep from telling her to mind her own business. Everybody—even Grandma and Uncle Edgar and Aunt Martha—seems to take it for granted that Rogers has a sort of—of first mortgage on me. Well, he hasn't—no one has."

David was speechless. He stared.

"You—and the others—might as well understand that," she went on. "I like Rogers, I like him very much, everyone likes him. But he and I are not en-

gaged to be married and—well, we are not going to be."

"But—but—why, look here, Em! Rogers thinks—I know he does—"

"I suppose perhaps he does, but he shouldn't."

"But I know he does. For years and years he has told me that he was going to marry you some day. Wasn't there any understanding between you—ever?"

Her color deepened. "Oh, possibly," she admitted. "Three years ago he—we—but I didn't give him any promise. If I said anything it wasn't more than just a 'perhaps.' And now— Oh," turning hastily away, "why did we ever get on *this* subject? Where are the cranberry vines? We must get some of those, too."

She moved off toward the green spread of hog cranberry on the next knoll. He followed her, his emotions curiously mixed. She was not going to marry Rogers, they were not even engaged. He ought to feel very badly about that, for Rogers' sake, but somehow— Poor old Rog, though; this was going to be a knockdown for him, spoil his homecoming and everything. But she was not engaged to him; apparently she was not even in love with him.

He thought perhaps he should put in some sort of plea for his brother; but he was pretty certain that it would be unwise to do so—just then, at any rate. And besides, she had said other things, even more

88

astonishing, not only in themselves but in what they implied.

How did she know his feelings concerning his humdrum part in the war, the wreck of his ambitions, and all that? He had been very careful to hide his chagrin and disappointment. No one else, even Father and Mother, had guessed, he was sure. She must have been thinking about him a great deal to read his mind like that. And she had said she was sorry for him. That was not pretense either, she meant it.

She had been thinking of him—of him, David Day. And why should she do that, unless— No, no! Careful, careful! Don't make a fool of yourself.

He knelt beside her on the carpet of wild cranberry vines, and they tugged and cut strenuously. They talked, but the conversation, every bit of it, was forced. It did not mean anything, all this about the church service and Bayport and the people in it, to him at any rate, and she did not seem greatly interested either. She said something about tomorrow being Christmas Day and that she could scarcely realize the fact. This led them back to the Christmas of ten years before, the one which she had said was the happiest she had ever known.

"Do you remember my losing the hair ribbon Grandma gave me?" she asked. "I didn't really think

I had lost it. I was almost sure you picked it up. And you had, hadn't you? When we met that evening in the upper hall I made you own up. You did look so red and guilty. It was funny."

She laughed. He smiled.

"I've got that ribbon yet," he said, quietly.

"You have? After all this long time?"

"Yes. I've always carried it with me. It has been on a good many voyages, that ribbon has."

"Oh."

"You gave it to me, you know. You don't mind my having kept it, do you?"

"Why—why, no, I suppose I don't. If you wanted it. Only— Don't you suppose we have picked enough of these things? We have more than we can use already, I am sure."

She rose. He remained where he was, his fingers twined in the cranberry vines.

"That was my best Christmas, too," he said, musingly. "And the end of it was best of all. When I realized you had given me that ribbon, given it to me and not to Rog— Whew! It didn't seem possible."

"Did you tell Rogers about it?"

"I've never told anybody."

"But we were just children."

"Um-hm. And little things please childish minds. I suppose that's what you were going to say?"

"No, of course I wasn't."

"It wasn't a little thing to me then—and it hasn't been since. I was a queer kid, I suppose, and I've never got over it. Never grown up, maybe."

"I asked you not to speak or think that way about yourself."

"Emily."

"Yes, Dave."

"It was straight, what you said about there being nothing between you and Rog?"

"Certainly it was."

Slowly he rose to his feet. He looked about him, then upward at the sky above the pine tops.

"Do you know," he observed, "I'm beginning to think perhaps it is clearing off. Is that a spot of sunshine up yonder?"

"Is it? I don't see any."

"Don't you? Maybe it's just in my head, but—but"—with a long breath—"it looks good, yes, it does."

"What *are* you talking about, Dave?"

"Sunshine.... Eh? Who's that?"

They were interrupted. If they had not been too preoccupied to notice it they must have heard, before this, the rattle and bump of carriage wheels and the thud of hoofs in the lane below the hill. Now they heard a voice. Thoph's voice, shouting their names.

"Dave! Emmie! Where be you? Hi!"

They answered the hail. A moment later Thoph came puffing and crashing through the bushes. He was wildly excited. His face was radiant, and he was waving his arms above his head.

"There you be at last, eh?" he panted. "Commenced to cal'late I'd never locate you. I never. Got news, I have! I says to Cap'n Edgar, says I: 'Dave and Em's got to hear this and I'm goin' to be the one to tell it to 'em.' Cap'n Edgar, he says: 'Can't it wait till they get home?' 'Wait nothin',' I told him. 'I'll hitch up and go after 'em now.' So—"

"Sshh! Lay to!" David ordered. "What is all this? What news?"

"About Cap'n Rog, that's what 'tis. And *sech* news! You know what he's done? His ship was took by a Reb privateer down below Hatteras some place and he got away from 'em in the fog and fetched her in safe. Yes, and he fetched a boat's crew of Rebs they put aboard her, too. Knocked 'em end-ways, Cap'n Rog and his men did, and fetched 'em into New York, prisoners. Got there night afore last. There was a letter for Cap'n Edgar in last night's mail, but the postmaster give it to that boy of Beriah Hallett's, and the everlastin' young-one put it in his pocket and forgot it till about an hour ago. There's a telegram from Rog, too. He's figgerin' to be home here tomorrow. He's a hero, that's what he is, a reg'lar hero, and the whole town'll be hurrahin' for him. Come on, come on! What you hangin' 'round here for? Heave ahead and get under way, why don't ye?"

3

THOPH'S PROPHECY was a true one. Before supper time that evening all Bayport was hurrahing for the good ship *Forward Light* and her commander. There had been so many disasters to northern shipping, so many vessels captured and burned by Confederate privateers and cruisers, that an exploit like Captain Rogers Day's was hailed as a triumph indeed, and especially in the captain's own town. When Thoph and David and Emily reached the house the sitting-room was already half-filled with neighbors and friends, and the jubilee was in full blast. The basketfull of evergreen and hog cranberry remained on the back of the two-seater, forgotten and neglected.

Captain Edgar had little more to add to Thoph's story. Rogers' letter had been short and gave only the barest facts. It was the fog dropping down on them so suddenly that did the trick, so Rogers said.

First time in all his going to sea that he had found a fog anything but a pesky nuisance. This time, though, it was a Godsend. Overpowering the boat's crew was easy enough. "There wasn't but a half dozen of them, and we had them three to one. The privateer wasn't a regular armed cruiser, like the *Alabama* or *Florida*, just a hit or miss outfit getting by the blockade on the chances of picking up a stray prize, I guess. We were lucky, that is about what it amounts to."

Lucky or not, Bayport was proud of its native son and intent upon doing him honor. The railroad had pushed itself as far down the Cape as Yarmouth by this time, and it was at Yarmouth that Rogers was scheduled to arrive at noon, or thereabouts, on the following day, Christmas Day. Already plans were on foot to meet him there.

All that evening more neighbors and friends came pouring in and, although the majority went away by ten, having preparations to make for the holiday, a few remained until midnight. An impromptu committee was formed and plans for the reception hurriedly made. Captain Elkanah Thomson, who had made a fortune in Australia, at the time of the Ballarat gold strike, and was the community's wealthiest citizen, owned a four-in-hand coach, a "tally-ho," which his sons and daughters and their children—

city dwellers, all of them—sported during the summer months. Captain Elkanah offered the tally-ho as the triumphal chariot in which the hero was to ride. A dozen buggies and carryalls were to follow in the procession. All flags along the main road—those not flying already—must be hoisted and the church bells rung when the parade came in sight. Bayport had no band of its own, but Sylvester Tidditt owned a bugle —veteran of the Mexican War—and that and the coach horn would have to serve for music.

The Day family retired at one or thereabouts, weary but very happy. David and Emily had had no opportunity to speak to each other, except in the general hullabaloo, for supper had been a hit or miss meal, Aurelia declaring she was so "sot up" over Cap'n Rog's doings she didn't know whether she was afoot or horseback. It was not until good nights were said and the young couple were on their way to their rooms on the second floor that they paused for an instant. Then Emily remembered.

"I suppose our Christmas greens are still out in the wagon," she said. "Oh, well, we may have time to arrange them in the morning, and if we don't it doesn't matter."

"Not a bit. Nothing matters except Rog's coming home. He'll make it Christmas for this family. We won't need any other decorations."

"No. Grandma and Auntie think we ought to save our presents until after dinner. He'll be here then, and we can have them all at the same time."

"Good idea! You'll ride to Yarmouth and back in the tally-ho, of course?"

"Why, I suppose so. And so will you."

"Yes. I understand they've booked passage for me. Don't know why. Rogers ought, by rights, to have that coach all to himself; he'll be the only one that people will want to look at. The rest of us will be nothing but that fifth wheel you hear about."

She looked up at him. "You don't mind, do you, Dave?" she asked.

"Mind? What do you mean?"

"Mind being the fifth wheel on your brother's coach."

"I should say not. Always have been, haven't I? And proud to be. Proud of him, too, mighty proud. Good old Rog!"

There was no trace of envy or bitterness in his tone. And yet she knew how he must feel, how he could not help but feel. Once more it was his brother who had succeeded, who had come through with flying colors, who would be praised and exalted. Whereas he, David, had, in his own estimation, failed miserably. There had been no public reception when he came home, no cheers, no hero worship.

She sighed. "You are pretty fine, Dave," she said. "You don't think so, but you are."

"Fine! Me?"

"Yes, you! And Rogers is just what you called him, the lucky one of the family."

"Oh, no, no! He's earned what is coming to him, every bit of it.... Emily?"

"Yes, what is it?"

"What you said this afternoon. I've been thinking about it a good deal. You didn't really mean it, of course. You'll be the first one he'll look for when he gets off that train. If—"

She lifted her hand. "Oh, hush!" she ordered. "You are— But there, good night."

97

4

HE TRAIN was only a half hour late at Yarmouth, an unusual circumstance at that period, and Captain Rogers Day's expression, when he stepped from the rear car and saw the gay procession drawn up by the platform, was something to remember. Rogers was not often at a loss for words, but he was just then. The condition did not endure, however. After the first shock he was his own hearty, good-natured, easy self again, shaking hands, laughing, thumping dignified Captain Elkanah on the back and exclaiming over the grandeur of the tally-ho.

"Feel as if I was running for office, or something," he declared. "If you expect me to make a speech, though, you're way off the course. That's one thing I won't do. Ah, Mother! Hello, Father! Ahoy there, Davie, boy! And—what? Why, Emmie! Well, well, you're a landfall for a sailor, I'll tell all hands! Let me look at you. . . . No, no, Cap'n Elkanah, if I've got to roost up there on the quarter-deck she's got to be there, too. Up with you, Em! That's right, that's the girl!"

So, on the highest seat of the tally-ho, that just above the one occupied by the Thomson coachman, he was enthroned. His mother was at his left hand and Emily at his right, with Captain Edgar and David in front with the driver. This was not exactly the seating arrangement which the committee had planned, but Rogers characteristically asked no one's advice, and this was not the time to contradict him. The coachman cracked his whip, the bugle blared, the four bewildered horses lifted their hoofs, the procession started.

And so they brought him home. Even in Denboro, the town between Yarmouth and Bayport, there were flags flying and people at their gates to cheer, and in Bayport itself everyone had turned out, leaving Christmas dinners to grow cold on the tables. They delivered him at the entrance to the Day driveway, and Thoph and Aurelia, both dressed in their finest, were there to greet him. He playfully punched Thoph in the middle of his Sunday shirt-bosom, kissed Aurelia and told her she was getting handsomer every minute, and, after a word of thanks to Captain Elkanah and the others of his escort, moved toward the side door, his mother clinging to his arm.

On the threshold he paused and turned.

"Can't tell you how I feel about all this," he shouted. "I'll try to by and by, though. Just now all I can say is that you are the finest people in the best town on earth. I've seen my share of other towns, here, there and yonder, and I know what I'm talking about. Thanks—and three cheers for Bayport!"

The Christmas dinner was strictly a family affair, for Captain Edgar and his wife had declared they were going to have their boy to themselves for so much of the day, at least. Aunt Desire was present, and the jollity and jubilation had their customary effect upon her spirits. She spoke feelingly of Christmases she had known when she was young and poor dear Judah was with her, asked for hot water when the cider was passed, and, as Captain Edgar said to Martha afterwards, was "swabbing her headlights" with her handkerchief at two-minute intervals. As this was her usual condition during almost any festivity, it was not permitted to wet-blanket this one.

Aurelia's comment to Thoph in the kitchen summed it up. "Needn't worry about her," snapped Aurelia. "She's havin' a good time. Only place she'd be better contented at is a funeral. I never in my life see anybody like her, and I have hopes that I never shall."

Thoph, a turkey wing between his thumb and finger, chuckled. "She reminds me of Elnathan Peters," he observed. "Elnathan's notion of a high old time was to drink rum enough to make him cry. When he was holdin' his head in his hands and cryin'

like a young-one everybody knew he was com-
mencin' to be happy."

The afternoon was a continuation of the morning
reception. More neighbors and friends, more hand-
shaking and back-slapping, more toasts and cheers
for Captain Rogers Day, the hero. Jeddie and his
mother drove over from Denboro, remained to have
supper with the family and for an hour or two in
the evening. Rogers was asked to tell the story of
his escape from the privateers over and over. He
announced that he guessed he would have it set to
music so that he could sing it. "That would be a
change, anyhow," he added.

5

I T WAS after eleven when Aunt Desire suddenly
announced that she was going home. No, she
wasn't going to stay all night. She was much
obliged to them, but all this racket and clickety-clack
was too much for her nerves, and she was going back
to her own house and her own bed. "You don't want
a poor lone widow woman moping around with you,
nobody does. The fitting place for me is by myself,
and that's where I ought to be, and mean to be, till

I'm took to the graveyard. If somebody will get word to the livery-stable they'll send a team for me."

Of course there was much protest, but she was firm. Captain Edgar declared that the livery-stable idea was ridiculous and that, if she was determined to go, Thoph would harness up and drive her home. Then David put in a word.

"Never mind Thoph, Aunt Desire," he said. "I'll drive you home. I'd like to. My head needs cooling off, too."

He went out to the barn, harnessed the horse, backed him into the buggy and, with Aunt Desire as passenger, drove out of the yard. The drive was not a cheerful excursion, although, fortunately, not a long one. Aunt Desire lived in West Bayport and he delivered her safely at her door. She urged him to come in. "I'll make you some nice hot ginger tea to take the chill off," she added. "No, come to think of it, I'm all out of ginger, forgot to send for it to the store, but I've got composition in the buttery, and composition tea is pretty nigh as good when it's made right. It's been such a comfort to me, when I'm all sole alone here, composition tea has."

David declined the composition tea, said good night and started for home. It was a clear starlit night, not too cold, and he leaned back on the buggy seat and let the horse jog on at his own gait. He had much to think about, and his thoughts were a curious mixture. Emily—himself—and Rogers. If she meant what she said—

Careful, careful, careful! Rogers was his brother, of whose success he had been so proud, whom he had worshiped all his life. There was such a thing as loyalty, there had to be.

The horse's jog slowed to a walk and a very deliberate walk at that. When David came out of his dream the animal was turning into the Day driveway. The lights in the parlor were extinguished and the lamp in the sitting-room was turned low. He must have been gone a long while and the guests had departed. Had all the family gone to bed? Probably; it had been a tiring day.

The horse was in his stall, the buggy safely in the carriage house, and David, lantern in hand, moved toward the barn door. He raised the lantern and was about to blow it out, when someone spoke his name. He turned quickly.

"Why, Em!" he exclaimed.

She was standing in the doorway.

"What are you out here for?" he asked. "Is anything the matter?"

She did not answer. He lifted the lantern until its light shone upon her face. She had been crying; there were tears in her eyes at that moment.

"Emily!" he cried. He sat the lantern down upon the floor and took a step toward her. "Emily, what is it?"

She spoke then. "Oh, Dave," she whispered, "I had to see you. I had just gone to my room and I saw the light in the barn. I am afraid. It seemed to me that I must see you right away and tell you before—before he did."

"He? Who?"

"Rogers. He and I have had a dreadful scene. He called me back to the sitting-room after the others had gone upstairs and—and—oh, how can I tell you? He—"

She was on the point of breaking down, but he seized her hand in his. "Steady, Em, steady!" he urged. "You can't stop now. You've got to tell me. You and Rog have—what?"

"We have—we have had an understanding. That is, I tried to make him understand, I tried to be as kind and—and considerate as I could, but I had to tell him the truth. It couldn't go on. I couldn't let him take everything for granted, it wasn't right or fair. So, when he made me wait there in the sitting-room and when he—he—"

"Easy, Emily, easy! Steady as she is. I guess likely I see what you mean. You told Rogers what you told

me yesterday, up there in the woods. You told him you weren't going to marry him."

"Yes."

"Pretty tough on the old boy. Took it hard, of course?"

"*Hard!* Why—"

"Yes, yes, I know. But if you made him understand—if you explained that you'd tried but you couldn't care for him enough to be his wife, why—well, he wouldn't want you to be. Nobody would."

"Oh, Dave, Dave! You are the one who doesn't understand. He did want me to be. He wouldn't listen. Just laughed, at first, and then, when I made it plain that I meant what I said, he was furious. He said things—dreadful things. And I lost my temper and I— Oh, Dave, that's why I had to see you before you saw him. You two mustn't quarrel. If you do I'll be responsible and I couldn't bear that. I couldn't!"

"Now, now, Emily. Why should Rog and I quarrel? He doesn't blame me for anything, does he?"

She was crying again, silently. He put his arm about her. "There's something more that I haven't got yet," he said slowly. "There must be. Emily, tell me the whole of it. Everything, if you can."

She drew a long breath. "I can't tell you," she protested. "Only he asked me if there was anyone else and I—I was very angry—and I said—"

"You said there was?"

"Yes, I did."

"But who—oh, good Lord! You don't mean—Emily, you can't mean that—that I—I—"

She was sobbing hysterically. He took her in his arms and tried to look down into her face, but she kept it hidden.

"Emily," he begged, "is that it? I—it doesn't seem possible. If it is— Oh, don't you see you *must* tell me? Emily!"

She did not answer. He tried again.

"Oh, Emily," he pleaded, brokenly. "I—oh, good Lord, I never meant to say it; I meant nobody should ever know, but if— You see, I've been in love with you ever since—ever since always, I guess. Only I thought you belonged to Rog, and so I had to—to cover it up. You see why, don't you? But now, if— if— Oh, I'm crazy, of course! Don't pay any attention to me."

She looked up then, and when she spoke her tone was halfway between tears and laughter.

"Oh, Dave, dear," she whispered, "I am sure there is nobody else like you in this world. If you weren't you, it would have happened long ago. I have done everything but propose to you and—and now I've done that. I don't care, though. But, Dave, are you sure—?"

6

HE WAS HOPING that his brother might be in bed and asleep when, a half hour later, he entered their room, the room they had shared as boys. Emily's last word had been the whispered plea that he would remember the promise he had made her.

"There is going to be trouble, dreadful trouble, I know," she said. "I didn't tell him how I felt about —about you, but I am sure he suspects. You won't quarrel with him, will you, dear? No matter what he says you mustn't do that. Promise me."

So David had promised. Goodness knew he had no wish to quarrel with his brother. His feeling toward the latter was a deep and sincere pity, and his affection for him greater than ever, if that were possible.

Rogers was not in bed. He was sitting in the chair by the table. As David entered he rose, and his first words proved that the trouble Emily had foreseen was at hand.

"Well?" he growled. "Here you are, finally. I've been waiting for you. It's about time you and I talked things out together. Just about time. What have you been up to behind my back, eh?"

David tried to smile. "What's all this, Rog?" he

asked. "This behind your back stuff? What do you mean?"

"You know cussed well what I mean. Course you do. A look at you is enough to prove it; you look as mean and sneaking as a wharf rat this minute. Come, come! Wipe that silly smirk off your mouth and face the music, if you've got any backbone in you—which I doubt."

"All right, Rog. Go on with your music. I'm facing it.... Just a minute, though; let me say this. I do know what you mean, or suppose I do; but you're wrong when you call me a sneak. I haven't done anything underhanded, I haven't worked against you. I've done my best to help things along for you. You may not believe it, but it is true. What has happened just did happen, that's all. No one is to blame. I'm mighty sorry—sorry for you, I mean."

"Shut up! You make me sick. A devil of a brother you are. Look here, are you and that—that damned—"

"Easy, Rog."

"Easy nothing! I'll call her what she is, and I'd like to see anybody try to stop me. She was engaged to me, wasn't she? You knew she was, didn't you?"

"She says she wasn't. She says—"

"I don't give a darn what she says. She's a—"

"Careful, careful! Say what you want to to me and I'll answer with the truth and nothing but the truth. Let's stick to ourselves and leave her out of it."

"Bah! Is she going to marry you?"

"I— Yes, I hope so."

"Ah ha!"—with a triumphant sneer—"I thought as much. She wouldn't give me the name of the sneak that cut me out, but I guessed. Oh, I'm not quite a fool. I've seen her look at you and you at her a half dozen times today. I *thought* she wasn't as glad as the rest of 'em to see me when I got home. And so I decided that, before I turned in, I'd get her alone and find out how matters stood. Well, I found out most of it and now you've told me the rest. You underhanded—"

"There, there! Calling names won't get us anywhere, Rog."

"What will? A fight? If that's what you want I'll oblige you and welcome. Right here or outdoors or anywhere you say. I'd ask nothing better than to have her see you after I got through with you. *Is* there any sand in your craw? If there is prove it."

David bit his lip. This was hard to bear. He ought to make allowances; poor old Rog was crazy mad and not responsible just now, but— And yet, there was that promise.

"I won't fight you, Rog," he said. "And there is no use talking to you till you calm down. You'll just have to take my word that there has been no working behind your back, nothing of that kind. I've cared for Emmie ever since I first saw her, I guess, and it turns out she's felt the same way about me. I've never let her know it, kept still and away from her on your account. It's only now, today, that we—that—"

"Oh, avast heaving! Cut out the lies— Will you fight or are you scared to?"

He had been passing up and down the room. Now there came a tap on the bedroom door.

"Boys!" It was Mrs. Day's voice. "Rogers! Dave! What *is* going on up here? You are making noise enough to wake the neighbors. Don't you realize it is almost three o'clock. Aren't you *ever* going to bed?"

David answered. "Yes, Mother," he said. "We're turning in now. Sorry we disturbed you. Good night."

They waited until they were sure she had gone back to her own room. Then, it was Rogers who spoke first.

"Humph!" he said, gruffly. "She's right, I suppose. No use advertising the rotten mess. Tomorrow— well, we'll see."

He said not another word that night, nor did David. In the morning, however, Rogers spoke once more, and his speech was coldly deliberate and final.

"Look here," he ordered. "I've been thinking it

over and I've come to the conclusion that we can't give this out for all Bayport to cackle over. And we don't want to upset the old folks either. I'll have to say yes and no to you once in a while for appearances' sake—and to her, too, damn her. But I haven't changed my opinion of you both and I never shall. Keep out of my sight for good and all. I'm through with you and her—through. Understand that and don't ever forget it."

Only the day before—so David reflected as he dressed—he and Emily had wished each other a Merry Christmas. Well, in one respect it had been a marvelous, a glorious Christmas for both of them, the beginning of life.

But so far as the old life was concerned, his life in which Rogers had played so wonderful a part, it was the end. And what an end!

PART THREE

The Seventies

PART THREE: THE SEVENTIES

I

THE SHIP *Sunrise*, David Day, commander, Briggs and Farnsworth of Boston, owners, was moving lazily, altogether too lazily, on a smooth sea. The wind was light, what there was of it coming in puffs. She was out of the southeast "trades" and in what the sailors used to call the "Horse Latitudes," and her progress was provokingly slow.

Captain David Day was impatient and more than a little worried. The *Sunrise* was homeward bound, from Melbourne to Boston, and the voyage had been a trying one. Good weather at its beginning, followed by a long stretch of head winds and calms which made the days and weeks seem endless. At last Cape Horn and an easy passage around that tricky corner, and then, when the trouble, or the worst of it, should have been over, another season of almost no wind and flat, greasy seas. Even the "trades" had not blown as they should. The *Sunrise* was already overdue at her home port; she should have been there before this. It was the most irritating voyage in Captain Day's seagoing experience and particularly irritating and worrisome because of his anxiety concerning Emily. And yet, it had not seemed as if they were taking chances. With ordinary luck, with ordinary winds and weather at the season of the year, she would have been safe at home by the time the baby was born.

He had figured—he had the right to figure—allowing for all ordinary delays, on making Boston by December first. Now it was December twentieth, Christmas only five days off, and look where they were!

After the war was over he had gone back to the merchant marine and had been fortunate in obtaining a command almost at once. Northern business was picking up again, and captains were needed. As soon as he signed articles he returned to Bayport, and he and Emily were married. It was a quiet wedding at the old home, with all the family present except Rogers. Rogers was on the high seas at the time, but had he been ashore he would not have attended. Rogers' feeling toward his brother had not changed since his expression of it the morning after that fateful Christmas Day when he learned that Dave, and not he, was to marry Emily Haynes. Nearly eight years ago, that was.

True to his word, except for the barest civilities when the family were present, he had not spoken to either of them, nor had he written or communicated in any way. Captain Edgar and his wife learned of the trouble—it could not be long hidden from them, of course—and they were greatly disturbed, but nothing could be done. They did not blame David or Emily; they felt very badly about the break in the family, but—well, Rogers was Rogers and, when his mind was made up, attempts to change it were usually unavailing and often only made matters worse.

"It will all come right some day, David, I'm sure it will," declared Martha. "I only hope your father and I live to see it, that's all. And we are so sorry for you, Dave, dear. You and Rogers were such *real* brothers always, if you know what I mean. Don't give up hope. We shan't."

David had not seen Rogers since the fortnight after their quarrel, when, feeling sufficiently strong and well again, he had gone back to his transport. Rogers had sailed from New York soon afterward. During the years never once, either by chance or design, had he been at home while his younger brother was there. From the family and from their letters David learned that Rogers was well and successful. His voyages, it seemed, were always "lucky," his personal ventures profitable, and his reputation as a sea captain high. In

Mother's most recent letter to David and Emily, received while the *Sunrise* was in Melbourne, she stated that Rogers had been at home for a week or two and was in high spirits. He was still in command of the old *Forward Light*, in the New York and San Francisco trade, but his owners were building a fine new vessel, and she was expected to be ready soon. When she was, Rogers was to command her.

"Father and I were in hopes," so Martha wrote, "that Rogers might forget Emily and perhaps fall in love with someone else and be married, but he never mentions having any such idea. I am afraid he will always be a bachelor, and it is too bad, for the right kind of wife would be a help to him. He mustn't have his own way *all* the time; that isn't good for *any*body."

It was not of his brother, however, nor of the latter's affairs, that Captain David was thinking as he walked the quarter-deck of the *Sunrise* that December morning. The calm sea and the idly flapping sails, although they were tormentingly distressing, were of secondary interest just then. His thoughts were below in the cabin and, at that moment, the object of them came up the companion.

"Oh, Dave," exclaimed Emily, as she reached his side, "what a lovely day! Another lovely day."

David grunted impatiently. "Too darned lovely, that's the trouble with it," he declared. "I'm getting so that I'd almost be glad to shake hands with a typhoon, if it would start us going somewhere." Then he added, anxiously, "How are you feeling, Em?"

She smiled. "Oh, pretty well. You mustn't worry about me, you know. You promised me you wouldn't."

"Humph! You are the one thing I really worry about. If you weren't aboard—"

She did not let him finish the sentence. "Hush!" she broke in. "Where else should I be? Besides, if I were at home, and your ship overdue and I waiting and waiting—well, do you think I should be happy there?"

"Maybe not, but I would be considerable happier —considering. At least you would be where there were women and—and doctors and nurses. Lord, Lord! All I can think of is suppose—suppose it should happen before we make port. Nobody but me. And what good would I be?"

She patted his arm. "It is going to be all right," she whispered. "I am sure it will. And even if it wasn't, I had rather be with you than anywhere else."

"I shouldn't have let you come."

"Would you have left me in Melbourne? You couldn't have, because I wouldn't have let you sail without me. I remember hearing your mother say— before we were married, it was—that a woman who married a sea captain must be willing and glad to spend her days and nights on salt water. 'It is the only way she can be with her husband, and if she doesn't want to be with him she had better not have married him.'"

"I know. Maybe you would have been better off if you hadn't married me. When I think of what may happen—"

"Hush! Don't be silly. Good morning, Mr. Cobb."

The first mate, a burly young fellow, bearded, as was the fashion in those days, and with his cap tilted toward his left eyebrow, touched his cap visor with his forefinger.

"Morning, Mrs. Day," he said. Then, addressing her husband: "She's just about moving and that's all, sir. Not much more than steerage way. I thought before I turned in that it might breeze on by sun-up, but it hasn't, not yet."

Captain Day nodded. "The glass is falling a little," he said. "That may mean something, perhaps. This sort of thing can't last forever. Or," he added gloomily, "I shouldn't think it could."

The mate observed that somebody had crossed their fingers on this voyage, he guessed. He went forward to see that the men, some of whom were swabbing decks and others polishing brass, were sticking to their jobs. Emily went to the cabin for her sewing and came up again to sit by her husband in the sun-

shine. The small garment she was at work upon caught David's eye and was one more, and quite unnecessary, reminder of the passage of time and the need of reaching port. He stifled a groan. He must get her home in time; he must. But the time was very near. He knew it and so did she, although she never spoke of it unless he did.

He glanced upward at the flapping sails and then out over the lazily heaving sea. Off in the southwest the sky was, as he would have said, "smurring up" a trifle. The horizon was not as clear.... No clouds, but an odd, reddish-brown haze low down along the sea line. A change of weather? Wind was what they needed and plenty of it, but— He went below once more to take another look at the barometer. It was still falling.

By afternoon it had fallen still more. The calm continued, but now the haze in the western sky had deepened to a slate color with a tinge of brassy yellow along the upper edges.

"What do you make of it, Mister?" he asked the mate, who was standing by the rail.

"Don't know, sir. Fuzziest looking mess I ever saw. We're in for something, I guess, but I'm not sure what. Glass is going down like a lead weight down a greased pole."

"I know. Well, better get ready for it, I suppose.

I hate to shorten, but I'm afraid we'll have to. Take in the light stuff and see that everything on deck is lashed."

"Aye, aye, sir. Double gaskets?"

"Might as well, while you're about it. Lord A'mighty! We've been whistling for a wind and couldn't raise a breath. Now it'll come in a heap, I presume likely. Well, get at it."

Mr. Cobb turned to obey and then turned back. He hesitated.

"What is it?" asked David.

"Why—nothing, Cap'n, only—only I was just hoping it wouldn't be too bad. Kind of—of tough on your wife, that's all. None of my business, sir, only—"

"I know. Good God, don't I know it! Get going! Lively now!"

The mate bellowed his orders. The crew raced aloft. The upper sails were furled and secured with double gaskets, instead of the fair-weather singles. All loose or movable articles in the waist and forward were secured with lashings. The *Sunrise*, under her lower canvas, was moving even slower than before, if that were possible. Along the westward and southern horizon the slaty sky was now almost black. The barometer was still falling.

"Better turn in, Emmie," counseled David, as he

came down for supper. "We're in for dirty weather; how dirty I don't know."

He left her in the stateroom and hurried on deck. Bradley, the second mate, was calling from the top of the companion stairs.

"She's coming, Cap'n," he shouted, "and she's a hellion, by the looks of her."

David took one look in the direction toward which the second mate was pointing. Where the ship lay the sea was as smooth as it had been, but a mile or two to windward was an advancing line of black and white water, rushing down upon them. His conscience smote him for lingering so long below. He should have known better. No excuse for neglecting duty, no matter—

"Stand by!" he roared. "Extra hand to the wheel here."

The extra hand was there already; good mates and good seamen, those mates of his.

"Keep her up into it," he ordered. "Don't let her fall off. Hang on now. Here it comes!"

It came with the thundering rush of an avalanche. The blast struck the ship like a thump from a giant's fist. She heeled down and down, then righted, reeling and staggering, but game. A sea washed over her amidships, tearing off a section of the sail like, as Mr. Cobb said afterward, "ripping the edge off the cover of a wet pasteboard box." Another and another followed it. The shrieking wind tore the topgallant sail from its fastenings, even the double gaskets not being able to hold it, and ripped it to streaming ribbons. The fight was on.

All night it continued. The tail end of a tropical hurricane it was, but, being fortunately only the tail end and not the center, the good ship *Sunrise* held her own and, although battered and bruised and crippled, was still alive and bravely battling when a dark morning broke over a gray and whitely frothing sea. The wind had, momentarily at least, abated a trifle, and the glass, although still very low, had not fallen in the last hour.

Cobb, a red-stained handkerchief tied across his forehead—he had been hit by a flying rope's end and knocked off his pins—wiped the salt from his eyes. "Well," he observed, "we're on top of water yet, and that's something. How's your lady standing it, sir?"

"Last time I went below to speak with her—an hour or so ago that was—she said she was all right. I don't see how she can be."

"Nor I neither. She's a—a—"

Apparently he could not think of an adequate word to express his admiration of Mrs. Day, so he gave up trying to do so. Instead he added: "How you making it, yourself, Cap'n? Between up here and down there you must have had a devil of a night:"

"Guess we've all had one, and I'm afraid the fun isn't all over yet. What's the damage so far? Anybody missing or hurt?"

"Nobody missing, so far as I can learn. Mr. Bradley's got a bad leg. Chucked end over end into the scuppers, he was, by one of those first seas. Wonder he didn't go overboard. Our boats are stove, I'm afraid, and we've lost all our top canvas; but of course I can't tell yet how bad off we are."

"Don't try. Keep her about as she is and look out for things as well as you can. I'm going below again for a few minutes, but I'll be right up."

"My respects to the lady, sir. Tell her we're through with the main circus. The rest of it'll be only the side-show—that is, I'm hoping 'twill."

The side-show was bad enough. The *Sunrise*, under her scraps of sail, was laboriously climbing the hills of water or slipping tipsily down their slopes. Her waist was a tangle of snarled rope and broken fragments of wood. Every once in a while a sea swept across it, and the men, clinging to the hastily rigged life lines, were knee-deep in water. But after each ducking she rose with a buoyancy which was encouraging, and the mate reported that she did not seem to be leaking a drop.

"Yes, she'll weather it, I'd say likely," observed David, with a satisfied nod. "No worse than this and she'll come through, Mister."

"Bet your life she will, sir. She's a tough old girl for her age. I wouldn't swap her for some of them they're sending off the ways since the war. She was built to stick together and, by Judas, she's sticking!"

The cabin was fairly dry—surprisingly dry, considering—and the stateroom in which Emily lay, lashed in her berth, was completely so. She smiled wanly when her husband entered, his oilskins and sou'wester running water like a sloping roof in a rain.

"Is everything all right, Dave?" she asked.

"All right so far and going to be better pretty soon, I believe. How is it with you, my girl?"

Again she tried to smile, but the attempt was so obvious that he could not but notice it. Holding by the edge of the berth to steady himself, he bent over her.

"How are you, Em?" he asked anxiously. "Tell the truth now."

She looked up at him and, as she did so, he saw her lips tighten and, in spite of her determination, she could not repress a moan.

"Em!" he cried. "Em, for heaven's sake—!"

She put her hand on his. "You'll have to be brave,

Dave dear," she whispered. "We shall both have to be. Dave, I—I'm afraid—"

He stared at her, aghast. "You don't mean—?" he gasped.

She nodded. "I'm afraid so," she said. "Yes, I—I'm sure of it now.... There, there, dear, don't be frightened. Don't look like that. It has happened often before like this—at sea, to other captains' wives, you know—and everything ended well. It will this time, I know it will. Dave, you *must* be brave. You must! Oh, I'm so sorry for you!"

"Sorry! For *me?* Oh, my God! And you're all so alone! *Emily!*"

2

ALL THAT DAY the *Sunrise*, in charge of her mates, one of them a cripple, fought her way through the slowly waning force of the storm. Her captain came on deck occasionally, gave whatever orders were necessary, looked at the compass, at the slowly rising barometer, asked a few questions, and went below again.

"You'll have to do the heft of it, Mister," he told the first mate. "You and Mr. Bradley. I'm not much good just now. Use your own judgment and hang on as well as you can, that's all."

"Aye, aye, sir. We'll hang on, don't you worry about us or the ship. How"—he hesitated, looking at his captain's haggard face—"how is everything—er—down yonder?"

"I don't know. I—I'm— Oh, well, call me if you need to. Only—"

"Only don't unless I do need to? Sure, I won't. Good luck, sir."

David left him, to go below once more. The second mate, limping stiffly, his damaged leg in improvised splints, came aft, clinging to the life line.

"The old man's pretty well shook, isn't he?" he said.

Mr. Cobb grunted. "Shook!" he repeated. "Wouldn't anybody be shook? A job like that on his hands and only a ship's doctor's book to give him his reckoning! Shook! Lord A'mighty! All hands know about it, of course?"

"Certain. All hands and the cook. They're sorry, too. Mighty fine skipper this crew's got, and they've got sense enough to appreciate it, for a wonder."

"Um-hm. Well, it's up to us, you and me, to keep things running right on deck here. You throw the fear of God into 'em for'ard."

"Huh! You needn't worry about that, Mister. But

I don't know's we need to be so tittered up. Not the first young-one to be born at sea by a consider'ble sight. Why, when I was fo'mast hand on the old *Highland*, out of New Bedford, the captain had his wife along and she—"

"All right. You can tell it by and by. Soon as it's smooth enough to risk, see about clearing that mess in the waist, will you?"

The clouds lightened late in the afternoon, and the western horizon showed a strip of gold below the gray. Four bells had just been struck when David Day next came on deck. Mr. Cobb looked at him sharply.

"Well, sir?" he asked.

David drew a hand across his forehead.

"It's a boy," he said. "Made port a while ago."

"Everything all right with—with both of 'em, Cap'n?"

David scarcely heard him. His face was a dead white beneath its tan and his eyes, as Cobb described them to Bradley, were "like two burnt holes in a blanket."

"Seems to be," he replied, absently. "Seems to be, but— Can't tell yet, I suppose. I'm hoping, that's all."

He shook his head, as if to clear it. He looked up and about him, at the shreds of canvas fluttering from the upper yards, at the littered and drenched decks, the broken rail, at the sea, the clouds and the western horizon.

"Hum," he murmured, "looks as if we were running out of it. Better be getting a little more sail on her pretty soon, Mister. I—" He sighed and gave it up. "You'll have to carry on a while yet, I'm afraid; I'm needed down there. . . . What time is it?"

Cobb told him. He sighed again.

"Kind of lost run of the time," he confessed. "Seems about a week. Be up again soon. You and the second have done a good job, Mr. Cobb. I shan't forget it, and I'll see that the owners don't, either."

The mate regarded him anxiously. "Don't you think you'd better turn in for a spell, Cap'n?" he suggested. "You look—you look as if you'd been through the wars, and that's a fact."

David's reply was prefaced by a grim laugh.

"Turn in! Turn in be darned! It's high time I turned out. I'm supposed to be the cap'n in charge of this craft, but nobody'd guess it from the way I've acted lately. . . . Well, there's another day coming."

3

THAT other day came and another after that. When the next morning dawned it found the *Sunrise* sliding briskly along over a blue and white sea, a good breeze pushing her, and a clear sky overhead. She was beginning to look like her old self again. Under the sharp eye of her captain, who was once more on deck and in active command, the wreckage in her waist had been cleared, spare canvas brought from the sail lockers and sent aloft, her decks scrubbed and her damaged cordage repaired or replaced. Captain Day had driven his men hard, but he had worked just as hard himself.

Second mate Bradley summed it up in his remark to Mr. Cobb. "The old man's squarin' up the lay-off he took," he observed with a wink. "Scared we'll think he's been loafing on his job and wants to show us who's who, I cal'late. Either that, or he's all puffed up about having a son of his own. Seen the kid yet, Mister? Who's it look like?"

"Looked more like a wizened-up gooseberry than anything else when I saw it. That was yesterday forenoon."

"Um-hm. Anybody'd know you was single. When you come to be dad to six of 'em, same as I am, you'd know that's the way they all look first off. Didn't say nothing about gooseberries to the old man, though, did you?"

"Think I'm a cussed fool? 'Cording to him it's a wonder. Proud as the Big Mogul, he is."

"Mother is getting along fine, so he tells me."

"She is. And she *is* a wonder. Say, this'll be a merry Christmas for both of 'em, won't it?"

"Humph! 'Tis Christmas Day, that's a fact. I forgot all about it. And fine weather and a fair breeze for Christmas presents. Well, they were coming to us, I'd say."

The conversation switched from social matters to others purely professional. The *Sunrise* had not come through the storm without scars. Besides damage to spars and rigging, two of her boats were stove by the seas and the other washed overboard and lost. The caps in the water butts had been loosened by the deck litter washing back and forth over them, and the drinking water itself contaminated. The food stores were also damaged. They needed flour and other essentials. Short rations and but a little water daily for each man, that meant, unless they should meet and speak with another vessel. Captain Day was hoping for that, and a lookout was posted aloft.

Below, in the cabin, David was finishing a rather scanty breakfast. The meal over, he stepped to the stateroom door, opened it cautiously, and peeped within. Emily was awake and spoke to him.

"Merry Christmas, Dave," she said.

Her husband whistled. "Well, well," he exclaimed, "it is Christmas, isn't it! First time I forgot Christmas since I was old enough to count, I guess. Merry Christmas to you, my girl, and a whole lot more of 'em to come. Sorry I haven't got a diamond tiara—that's what they call the things, isn't it?—for you, but that'll have to wait till we hit Boston. My will is good, but the jewelry shops in these latitudes are shut up. How are you feeling?"

"Oh, ever and ever so much better—and ever so much stronger. I haven't a Christmas present for you either, dear. I'm sorry. Yours must wait, too."

"Don't let that fret you. To have you safe and on the way up the ladder is Christmas enough for this particular salt-herring. And—why, say! What's the matter with me? We've got one present that beats 'em all! How is he hitting it off on his first Christmas?"

She smiled and turned back the fold of the blanket. David bent to scrutinize the tiny puckered face of his son.

"Merry Christmas, Cap'n Frederick," he whispered. "Getting to look more and more like his mother every breath he draws, isn't he?"

"Nonsense! He doesn't look like anyone yet, of

course. You mustn't make fun of him, Dave."

"Me? I'd as soon think of making fun of Admiral Farragut. Thought of a good middle name for him yet?"

It had been decided, months before, that, should the baby be a boy, he was to be named for Emily's father. Emily had insisted that he was to be Frederick David, but her husband, although inwardly delighted, pretended to demur. "Let's leave that for a spell," he urged. "Maybe he might live to hold it against us. Never cared much for David as a name, myself. Always reminded me of psalm-singing in meeting, when I was little and had to go."

So, as a joke, they pretended that the question of the "middle name" was still in abeyance. She smiled now at her husband's question.

"You know how I feel about that," she said, "but we won't argue about it—at present."

"I won't argue about anything, or ever find fault with my luck again. I'm too almighty thankful— Eh? Aye, aye! What is it?"

The steward was rapping on the stateroom door. "The mate wanted me to tell you there was a sail in sight, sir."

When David reached the deck the sail was just visible, a faint white blot on the northern skyline. Mr. Cobb was looking at it through the spyglass.

"Three-master, square-rigged, headed this way," he

141

said, handing the glass to the captain. David took it and looked long and carefully.

"We want to speak to her, whatever she is," he declared. "She can give us water, anyhow, and, if she's bound out, probably she can let us have some supplies."

"Hope she can spare some tobacco," muttered the mate. "There isn't enough aboard us to raise a smoke that would make a mosquito cough."

The course was set to cross the stranger's bows. She was coming on fast and, in an hour, was plainly visible. A fine, tall, full-rigged ship, most of her canvas spread, and flying through the water. David ordered a flag hoisted in the *Sunrise's* rigging and the weather clew of the mainsail hauled up, the usual signals in those days to signify a desire to speak.

"She's a Yankee, sir," said the first mate. "Flying the Stars and Stripes. Able-looking craft, isn't she?"

She was indeed, and beautiful to look at as she came on. David gave his orders, and the *Sunrise* luffed up to cross her course. Then, as the ships neared each other, both backed their main-topsails and lay almost still, rocking on the waves.

David stepped to the after-rail and raised his speaking trumpet to his lips.

"This is the ship *Sunrise*, of Boston, homeward bound from Australia," he hailed. "Struck by a gale four days ago and in need of water and stores. Can you spare them?"

"Aye, aye. Are you sending a boat?"

"Sorry, but I can't. Boats stove or lost in the gale."

"All right, I'll send mine over. What do you need?"

"Flour and water and tobacco. Little of everything, I guess. Medical supplies, too, if you have plenty on hand. Cap'n's wife has just had a baby born aboard here."

"What? A *baby*, did you say?"

"Yes. Born three days ago."

A momentary pause. Then, from the other ship: "Did you say you were the *Sunrise*, of Boston?"

"Aye, aye. That's right."

"What's your skipper's name?"

"Day."

Mr. Cobb, at his master's elbow, muttered impatiently. "Mighty fussy, he is, seems to me. Didn't trouble to tell us who *he* was. Can you make out her name, Cap'n?"

"Yes. She's the *Bold*—wait a minute: now I've got it—the *Bold Roamer*, or something like that."

"*Bold Roamer*, eh? Never heard of her before."

"Neither have I. Must be new, I guess; she looks it. . . . Well, come on, Roamer, lively, lively! What we want is to see that boat, not to hang around and gam."

143

The "gam" was apparently over, for there were signs of liveliness on the *Bold Roamer's* decks. A boat swung out on the davits. David watched for a moment or two, then went below to tell Emily the news.

"If she's what she looks to be, just out of port, she ought to be able to let us have something more than out of the regular mess," he told his wife. "Maybe there'll be some fruit—apples, anyhow. Perhaps they've got a chicken coop aboard. A fresh egg wouldn't be so bad for you just now; eh, Mrs. Day?"

"It would be nice, wouldn't it? But we'll be where we can get all those nice things pretty soon."

"Will if this weather holds. You and I will be eating Aurelia's mince pie before very long, I'm commencing to hope."

When he went on deck again the boat from the *Bold Roamer* was almost alongside the *Sunrise*. David stepped to the rail to look at her. Mr. Cobb was there before him.

"Far as I can see he hasn't brought a darned thing with him," he growled. "Nothing in her but the hands and the mate. He must have heard what you said, sir. We hear *him* all right. . . . What's the matter, Cap'n?"

David was staring at the approaching boat. He uttered an exclamation.

"That man in the stern of her!" he gasped. "The one at the tiller. He—he looks—"

"Eh? The mate, you mean? What about him, sir? Do you know him?"

"He isn't any mate. He—he is—"

"Yes, sir?"

David Day caught his breath, "He is my brother," he said, slowly. "Rogers! Good Lord above!"

The boat came up under the lee of the *Sunrise* and was made fast. The rowers pulled the oars in hand. The man in the stern clambered over the ship's rail. David came slowly forward to meet him.

4

WHAT SORT of a meeting would it be? The last time he had seen this brother of his— and that was seven, almost eight, years before—the latter had not so much as said good-by when they parted. Nor to any of the family, so far as David could learn, had he ever intimated that the old grudge was forgotten, that his feeling toward David or Emily had changed one iota. Well, the music must be faced and if the tune proved to be disagreeable it should not be his—David's—fault.

"Why, Rog!" he cried and held out his hand.

To his amazement Rogers did not avoid that hand. He took it in his own, squeezed it heartily, and, with the other, seized his brother's shoulder and shook him back and forth.

"Well, well!" he hailed. "Wonders'll never cease, eh? This is a high old place for you and me to run across each other; right spang in the middle of nowhere. You look as if seeing me had struck you all aback with your canvas flapping, as old Thoph used to tell about. Some surprised when you sighted me in the stern of that boat, maybe? Ha, ha!"

David's canvas was still flapping. He said something, but it was not coherent. Rogers went on:

"That's where I had the weather gage of you, boy," he explained. "Soon as you said this ship was the *Sunrise* and that a Day commanded her I knew who you must be. Pretty near fell down, I did. Couldn't trust to my ears, so I had to come myself and make certain. Here! Let me look at you."

He stepped back and inspected his brother from head to foot. "Just the same good-looking kid as ever," he crowed. "Little older, but almighty little, at that. Well, well! How do you keep that way?"

David tried to pull his shaken wits together. To meet his brother here on the high seas was miracle enough; but to be greeted by him in this fashion was even more amazing. This was the old Rogers. Just

as self-confident, just as breezy and jovially conde-
scending as he had been in the days when they were
boys. Not a scowl, not a trace of hate or resentment.
What did—what could it mean?

He laughed, but the laugh was rather ricketty.
"You could have knocked me overboard with a clew
line when I saw it was you," he stammered. "I can't
believe it yet."

"Simple enough. I'm on my way from New York
to California. Regular course and a great run so far.
But where did you come from?"

David began to speak of his voyage from Melbourne. Rogers interrupted before he had said more
than a few words. "That'll all keep till later," he
said. "Well, glad to see me, are you?"

"Don't think I was ever so glad to see anybody."

"Glad to see you, too. Wait a minute, though.
How about those stores? Didn't bring any with me.
Figure to send the boat back for 'em. Got a list of
what you want, have you?"

David admitted that he had no list, but could make
one if it was necessary.

"Bet your life it's necessary. According to what
you said when you hailed you've had a tough time.
...And what's this about a baby?"

They walked aft together. David told the story of
the storm and the birth of his son. Rogers seemed to

consider the baby a great joke. "Ho, ho!" he shouted. "I'm an uncle! Uncle Rog! Well, what do you think of that! How's Em getting on?"

He mentioned her name without the least embarrassment. Another miracle.

"She's picking up every minute. When I tell her who has come calling she'll be better yet. But I can't make it out—any of it. Where did you get that— what's-her-name?—*Bold Roamer* craft? What's become of the old *Forward Light?*"

The *Forward Light,* it seemed, was in dry dock for overhauling and refitting. The *Bold Roamer* was the new vessel Rogers' owners had ordered built, the one mentioned by Martha in her letter. "They promised her to me," said Rogers, "and they kept their word. She's a lady, too, from foot to bonnet. We've come from New York flying. If she can keep up this gait we'll come close to the record for the San Francisco run."

He was tremendously proud of his ship. David broke in on the chant of praise.

"I must go below and tell Emily about you," he said. "Won't be but a minute."

"Give her my love. *And* best respects to my nephew. Ho, ho! Say, can't I have a squint at him? First nephew I ever had, you know."

"Course you can. But—about those stores—"

He hastily jotted down the items on the back of an envelope taken from his pocket.

"Water and flour and tobacco we need most," he said. "Medicine and stuff for the doctor chest will help a lot, too. And, if you do have a little to spare in the fruit or fresh vegetable line, I could use them. Not for myself, understand; but Emily—"

"Sure, certain! Don't worry about that. This is the *Roamer's* first voyage and there was a send-off party aboard before we set sail. Em will figure she is having dinner at the Tremont House when she sees what I've got for her. You know what day this is, don't you?"

"Yes. But I didn't think of it till she wished me Merry Christmas a little while ago."

"All right, I'll see that you remember it for a while. Tell Em you're going to have company at that dinner. Sorry you aren't both in shape so that I could have you aboard the *Roamer;* I'd show you a *real* ship then. But, if you can't eat with me, what's the matter with my eating with you? Wind and sea as they are, we could luff around abreast each other for a week—that is, we could if it wasn't for my having to keep after that Frisco record. . . . See you later. Got to go back and load up that boat."

He hurried forward, leaving his brother in a sort of daze. Of course there was no real reason why Rogers should not dine with them. It was not at all unusual for the captain of one sailing ship, wind and weather permitting, to visit another captain on the high seas. Sometimes they shared a meal together, sometimes the purpose of the call was merely a social chat—"coming aboard for a gam," they used to term it. That was not strange, but that Rogers should accept their hospitality, even invite himself to partake of it, was, under the circumstances, bewilderingly strange.

Emily was as astonished as her husband had been at the discovery of their visitor's identity.

"It doesn't seem as if it could be," she declared. "With all the great ocean and all the vessels on it, that we should meet *his* ship and meet him! I can't believe it."

"Yes, it's odd enough, but 'most anything can happen on salt water."

"You say he doesn't seem to have any ill-feeling toward us at all?"

"Feeling? I give you my word I thought he was going to kiss me. Sent his love to you and—and— Oh, it beats all *my* going to sea! *I* give it up!"

Emily, too, gave it up. Neither could understand the change in Rogers' attitude toward them, and speculation got them nowhere. As Emily said, the reason—if there was any particular reason—did not really matter. The change was there, and it made her very happy.

"Now perhaps you and he can be what you used to be to each other. I am so glad. I have felt very badly about your quarrel. It was my fault, I know. You quarreled about me."

"*I* didn't quarrel; he was the one who wanted to fight. All I can think of is that it has been so long a time he has decided to forget and forgive. That isn't enough, though, not for Rog. He isn't the kind to forget or forgive either. There's something else, something we don't know about—yet."

The answer to their riddle was given just as the brothers were finishing dinner in the cabin of the *Sunrise.* Emily was not yet strong enough to come to the table, but she had her share of the good things Rogers had brought in her stateroom and the stateroom door was open. She could both see and hear.

It was, as Rogers boasted, a pretty fair average Christmas dinner, latitude and longitude considered. "Of course," he said, "it is too bad we couldn't invite the neighbors, but they're a long ways off and the going is pretty wet under foot."

There was a chicken—the *Bold Roamer* had a coop on board; potatoes, cabbage, cranberry sauce, hot biscuits, a plum duff, apples, nuts and raisins. Even some fruit cake, left over from the "send-off party." And, to make it a real celebration, Rogers produced a partially emptied bottle of port wine.

"Brought one full one," he said, "but that's for Em's use on the voyage home, so no trespassing allowed. This one, though—what there is of it—is for this dinner, and I'm calculating to have lot and share in it myself. There's three or four—what-d'ye-call-'em—toasts—I'm going to propose, so we'll have to do with short allowance for each one. About quarter of a glass, say. All ready? Here we go then!"

He lifted his glass and bowed solemnly in the direction of the stateroom door. "To Nephew Frederick Day and his mother. Merry Christmas to both of 'em and good luck all the way."

Emily, from her berth, called a "Thank you." Frederick, himself, inadvertently awakened, squawked and relapsed into slumber. Rogers, the self-appointed toastmaster, poured another spoonful of wine into his glass and again raised it.

"And now one to the home folks. Mother and Father and Grandmother, Lord bless 'em! Oh, yes, and not forgetting Aurelia and good old Thoph."

That toast was applauded and drunk with honors. Then Rogers poured another thimbleful for himself and David. "Oh, yes, Emmie," he insisted, "you'll have to be in on this, too, because I'm going to be 'specially slighted, if you don't. Fetch her glass, Dave. That's right. Now this is going to surprise you. I—well, you see—"

For the first time since boarding the *Sunrise* he did show slight symptoms of embarrassment. He even seemed a trifle sheepish, as he hesitated, but only for a moment.

"I'm going to ask you to drink this time," he went on, "to—to—well, a new member of the Day family. That is, she isn't a Day yet, but she's going to be soon as I make New York again, after my voyage out and back. Her name is Etta—er—Henrietta Bradshaw; her father is Samuel Bradshaw, one of my owners—the ones that built the *Bold Roamer* for me. And—well— to make it short—she's promised to marry a fellow by the first name of Rogers. So—"

David waited to hear no more. He jumped from his chair to rush around the table and thump his brother on the back. Emily called excitedly from the stateroom. Nephew Frederick woke again and lifted his voice with the others. It was an exciting climax to the little celebration.

Rogers told them all about it. Nothing sudden about it, in one way, he explained. He and the young lady had known each other for a good while. "Seen a good deal of her since I've been sailing for her father," he said. "Been up to their house for dinner and taken her out to theaters and shows. The other part of it, this marrying idea, well, that *was* sort of sudden, I suppose you might say. I'd been thinking about it, and I presume likely she had, but— Oh, well, you know how these things happen. We found out, that's all, and now we're going to sign articles. Here's her photograph. Brought it along from the *Roamer* to show you."

He produced the photograph from his pocket and proudly displayed it. Miss Bradshaw was a good-looking young woman, with dark eyes and a firm chin. "She looks as if she had a mind of her own," Emily told Dave afterwards. "She will give orders as well as take them, and that should be very good for Rogers, very good indeed."

It was evident that Rogers had no doubts concerning the wisdom of his selection. He spoke lengthily in praise of her looks, manner, and general desirability. The mystery of his change of heart toward his brother and Emily was a mystery no longer. He was off with the old love and very much on with the new. Quite characteristically, however, he did not once refer to the former or to the quarrel and long estrangement. He was a very happy man, and his companions there in the cabin of the *Sunrise* were equally happy. The cloud in the Day family's sky had blown away, and that sky was clear once more.

Rogers said good-by to Emily and went on deck. David lingered a moment, went into the stateroom and whispered to his wife. He had what he considered a brilliant idea. She did not seem to share his belief in its brilliancy.

"Do you really want to do that?" she asked.

"Eh? Why, I don't know. Just thought it might be a nice thing to do. It would tickle Rog, I shouldn't wonder. Of course, if you don't feel that way about it—"

"I don't."

"Don't, eh? Why?"

"Because—oh, Dave, dear, can't you see? Rogers has enough to tickle him, as you call it, already. A new ship, engaged to a rich girl, an assured future—everything he can possibly want or hope for. You haven't nearly as much—"

"Here, here! I've got all I want. Wouldn't change with him or anyone else in this world, I tell you that."

"Neither would I. But I don't think you should give up what I know you would like, and what I want so very much, for your brother's sake. So, unless you have really set your heart on it—"

"No, no. I haven't. Just a notion that came to me, that's all. To tell you the truth, I did feel kind of bad about doing it, but I thought—"

"I know. You thought about someone else and not yourself. That is your one bad habit, Dave."

The baby stirred and she bent over him.

"Lie still, pet," she murmured soothingly. "Don't worry. You are not going to be Frederick Rogers Day at all. You are Frederick David Day, just as your mother planned for you to be from the very beginning. . . . There"—turning to her husband—"hurry on deck or Rogers will be gone before you get there."

5

THE SUN was a fiery ball dropping toward the western horizon. The wind was fresh and steady. The *Sunrise*, all her canvas spread, was moving swiftly on her course. Far to the south, a white dot on the skyline, the *Bold Roamer* was moving even more swiftly in the opposite direction.

Captain David Day took the spyglass from his eye. Mr. Cobb, coming aft, climbed to the quarter-deck and touched his cap.

"Another Christmas 'most over, sir," he said. "Turned out to be a good one for us, after all, didn't it?"

"Yes. Men enjoy their dinner?"

"Don't know why they shouldn't. You ought to have seen 'em lay into the duff. Hope you and your lady and your brother enjoyed yourselves. Kind of odd meeting him, wasn't it?"

156

"Odd enough. I've known of things like it happening, but not very often."

"The second and I were talking about it. He recollected knowing two other brothers who ran across each other in mid-Atlantic one time. They hadn't seen each other for years—one being at sea while the other was ashore, you know—and then one day they spoke each other's vessel, just as you and your brother did today. Their name was Taylor, or seems to me 'twas."

"Yes. Well, I suppose my grandfather would say it was all planned by the powers above. Perhaps it was. I don't know."

The mate moved away. David took one more look through the glass. The *Bold Roamer's* topsails were barely visible now.

David drew a long breath. Christmas really must be what his father had declared it to be, the Day's lucky day. And today—this Christmas—was the luckiest of all. Emily rapidly gaining health and strength; their son, Frederick David Day—there was a thrill in that name, no use pretending there wasn't—below in the stateroom; the ship safely through the hurricane and with the promise of good weather for the remainder of the voyage; the long estrangement between Rogers and himself over and done with.

A lucky day! A Christmas Day to enter in red ink

in the log of his life—of all their lives.

He turned to the mate. "Well, Mister," he said, "things look promising. Good sea, wind where we want it and everything drawing. We'll put her nose in the home notch and keep it there, eh?"

Mr. Cobb's grin was broad.

"Aye, aye, sir!" he agreed. "Home she goes."